Y0-FCV-016

Recent books by Clark Coolidge:

Quartz Hearts (This, 1978)
Own Face (Angel Hair Books, 1978)
Smithsonian Depositions/Subject to a Film (Vehicle Editions, 1980)
A Geology (Potes & Poets Press, 1981)
American Ones (Tombouctou Books, 1981)
Research (Tuumba, 1982)

MINE: THE ONE THAT ENTERS THE STORIES

Clark Coolidge

The Figures
1982

Cover by Suzanne Hellmuth & Jock Reynolds.
Publication of this book was partially supported
by a grant from the National Endowment for the Arts.
The Figures, Great Barrington, Ma, 01230
Distributed by *Small Press Distribution, Bookslinger, Segue,*
and *Inland Book Company.*
Copyright © 1982 by Clark Coolidge
Second Printing, 1986
ISBN 0–935724–14–1

MINE: THE ONE THAT ENTERS THE STORIES

I

THE WORLD LOOKS LIKE it's upside down today. I mean, by that, there's nothing to repeat, at last. But that's, no doubt, not entirely true. The trees are all still standing there, no wind, and they're not at all like people as I saw somewhere the other day. Lots of what you read seems to go to make up one big anonymous voice, it's not really that you just can't remember exactly who said anything. Something in writing makes me want to get up, avoid, and walk around to no purpose. Perhaps this will be a big book of very little definition.

Where was I? Standing here sitting. Betwixt and bewhile. Turning around to see sun or moon on a last point of land. And could one make a sonnet of nothing but trees. No doubt later there would at least be a window somewhere. Trees are like clothes, they . . . No. From the point of a pen things stand for a time. As long as one goes on with it, going on being eventually to forget what one started out to do. I think of soap, alone, no use, for no reason in the world I can tell. Secrets are locked up everywhere in procedure. Tell me the time and I'll tell you an unkempt joke. The hours are like clouds, their coming and going directions obvious. But, as far as I can tell, writing, like its poor cousin speech, has no beginning.

Knowledge is useless, unless it is aggressive, using its secrets like swords. I have often seen the hacking variety, unclean, unstable, useful only for starting backfires. My palms itch and my back has been strained and she asks me where is the saw and I tell her I put it on the red settee on the porch. An epithet is a denying use of somebody's name.

But didn't I start out here to tell a story? Perhaps, the central start of any tale, as Beckett says. Mine is a shadow of tar boiled in thought till it is a horse approaching to kill you. Don't call up what you can't put down, as the old darker magic had it. But often enough mind and world get together on the old walling-off-of-choice operation and whatever could you have been thinking of. The light of day, the trees in lines, the recurring of dark as a solving.

I hate glancing across spines of books in rows. What they are is not so easily contained. I should dig a sub-basement here and make them all live down there in the dark. Deep in the world is a pitless pear, surrounded by cities of airless stone. How are the people there, and how do they view the pear. Do they ensure that any account of their life and bounds must rhyme? The steady congealing of losing one's way into frictionless art. Viewed by life on a float.

All books live in the dark anyway. Then they await the opening light of an eye, as in a child's garden movie? I can only take heart if pickled, of an artichoke that is. Is what true? The dreams in which I go about my same life as awake, the only thing different and of interest being the room it's all taking place in. Sometimes I suppose that my empathy is more with things than people anyway. Supposedly a terrible thing to say, think to admit. Perhaps of a day I'll take the right side. The night side in which all seems rightside up.

Chimneys seem more reputable in the mornings, therefore they are the property of dreams. You see birds come out of them sometimes. At nightfall they pour back in. Topless chimneys of my childhood, and vast vertical thundercloud masses turreted directly above my backyard. No sky has ever seemed so upwards since. Nor have I ever lain so planked down flat on my back in the grass of the absolute bottom floor of the world. Well, it's all too much, so much above me, as they said. And the world keeps consuming 'round, turning rind.

Bloody tigers and fang-high fences in my dreams. Horses with baggy pockets and rhymes for cast-away things. Iron laundry poles as the center of the earth. And when the mail got handed it would be warm in your hand. Nobody lived past their role in life. Movies so dark it seemed impossible you could see a thing. Or anywhere a place to think. I pretended I knew my name and they never forgot my seeming knowledge. The windows either blue, grey, or an absolute black.

To tell the tale, to wax unrepentant, to overlook the middle for all its ends, to form all cast out on the sea a lining, to wait until the glance all sufficiently watches. He lost the key with only the first name attached, all resultant pursuits for the nonce baseless. The agent assuming the guise leadless or is it pointless. However the threading I can well imagine. Battersea Bridge in the morning star.

Too often I worry about the world, I worry about a window. The world now as a blanket of thoughts blank. What do I think of what I do think blank. Or is it thought that strews the trees then returns to shake them. Not of persons. The liver and the gingerale and the poreless packages in passages awaiting trammel. The people that seem to walk in tune with lag notions, that cancel the brightness of the blue sky with blueness, that age things beyond their term with speech. Will I have to think about or further work my dreams if I turn to the next item of apparel. How did Henry James hold to all the crevices of his sentences, and how did he stand by what he thought to be his shortcomings. As Proust, to my mind, no need to, didn't.

The lights are on the fairway, the lines are teeming up to naught. The Labor Relation Squad grinds down the marble stairs of FiddleGut Canal. The three cats pausing there, each by its hand-dipped candle. The iron claw in the bone-and-plaster mansion-side. Perhaps the Sirens had no notion of Ulysses' passing. Only an error in repeating verse. The time it takes for things set together to adhere, said Joyce. But today the bones ring with air, only air.

Yesterday I painted the ceiling, today it's as bare as ever. When notion's focused close what's aligned and what gives. The rocks that were brought in the house proved short one. The shirt off my back made still. Turn on the radio, listen to the hours that hover in a caution of steel brads. The horse came over the bridge, why does that ring with a moon. And I take my hand off the switch and light the lamps. I'm not careful enough and I talk. That I bolt my food I cough up what loosens. I learn spelling and I smell. I lap up the lightning by a water that's loosening. I call the wall Latin, a pinball that's flat.

Apple towers. That's firm enough for a possible daytime. Then I examine my shit in the rock bowl for reddish trails. Then I think of Allen Ginsberg, the constant millions of poems. But the longer the work grows nameless. An astronomic ukelele. Ah, the venerable poet laughing all over the leaning place of yellow objects. He doesn't want to throttle the basket weave, he wants to bare the glass, attend the boring plectrums, seat all the peering trains in lead-bottom world. The standpoint is ever the period, says Creeley. The coins in the cashbox appointing blurry world. Enough of the word world, enough of seem and as if phrases, enough of the sermon on the mount no one heard clearly in the yellow gum wind anyway. Enough of anyway. Stop poetry and stuff candlesticks. Green back dollar bill of croaking cerebral Ray Charles on a cocked electric joystick. Better Stevie Wonder on skyshard chainsaw? Poetry without music another court of bliss. Don't stitch the numbers on the wetted side of your choppy plans.

Chainsaw blatter clogs the gunked up anyway mind today, old folks rolling the mildew log. Would my thoughts would come to a pretty pass, exact cobalt breezeway image of tooth among mesas blaring crimson. If I coil such glassy data enough will it critical up to independent shock transform? I smoke too many transitions anyway, bubble on the burnside mind. Sounds turn flaps and the cigarette's active point is a hole. I think to myself all the things within reach on jammy typewriter fading tattoo. But there are things in this world undercooked beyond thought, the clearest view the underworld. But I don't link any thing enough to stop it. And I lie as I love it. I have thongs in my mouth stand in for teeth tie up the view for others. Noticing the flattened slug ring on Miles' horn hand. Inking into the blue sky of far away blade chains. There is no youth, only variously light-soaked ignorances. Next to the corn wall a thorium tube.

Fits of writing, but how will it all haul hollow out. The eastern sky aflame with pitch, the western at noon under knees. And the separate rocks are green from pressure of dreaming. Dreams they will spur their grains into wheels of a sibilance leaning. Core all lashed across the backforest lawn. The fire is in the spine. The door is open on blade of a tree takes star ice. And all of my pages bead wooden. Then what be the story I was bound to tell?

When I started this and now, the morning is gone. There are ropes attached to the strained hips, haul on sonnets of Shakespeare. Must we heave our years along with our selves, Dali's pianos? I bring to you understanding of the true cancellations long past forgetting. Everything not said here of everlasting import. Try yourself out in a blue pair of olden shoes. Sixties art the colors of product shelved, lips bruised at gearloose hands. But Billie Holiday caulks the window in blossoming eggplant. That I throat honks in the morning, but I place myself past too fast. Now I see no roofs and have lost my youth aloft.

Now I'm going to once again drive past all the southern New England oat windows as in a spelling lesson. Where then those persons of arm loads will curve into snails and match. And underneath each television is a sample stone of this region. The poem that merely goes by is detectively simple. Three lines past one point and I lost my mind for a minute. Lost sight of birds, lost alphabet cards, lost subsidiary thing with the hole in the middle. The album car. A coining of wheat to spin in your ear. A factory lover, a lump to the giver. A whitewash down under the eerie loaves of the Rumpleskin Brewery. The walk back to the meal under the odd domed hill too late for weed.

Each time all the theories of poetry amount up to a lapse under the slick between every two words. More important the metallic ring at each tap says this typewriter may soon fall apart. And between those nothing but, as the piano player fingers, my heart. A lamp on the couch in the afternoon small. That poetry is a dwindle. But I do want to say something as a speaker, an alarming of masses, a cough in the corridor between cases. But these people are cramps, even to the heels of their volumes. As I march past across collided New England to gain smile at a winter-heated hay. The girlfriends' sizes have come in the post today, literal bumps. Each side of toast the beginning of a story. Story of scarcity bristlings.

Meanwhile I sat here coded. Stared off in the light a stranded apparition. And the guy says to me, he says, if you look down into this shaftway here you'll see the steely beckon of an orange coming. But I don't believe in the chance tattle, only in stationary dreams where the borders keep you edgy for news. As for instance, the salamander should report in the poem on fire. Would you see him sneer at any worry on housing? Your name is the precise settle of lights on anything spinning.

Today the sun is as wide as a blue car register, but the cat tray in the basement still smells of a recent movement. No matter the writing erratic long as it stays down. Made an error right in my face. Later the long cards were brought in ready for my filching, I mean my signature. They wanted the strokes rhymed to the timing of those violent tube lights. I couldn't though ended up I stubbed. The cat over again. The miles to go in one furl steering motion. Then I put on my clocks and went instairs.

In a word, the mercenary tweeds. That I possess the manifold poems of everybody sun-hot in the bright volumes of the weeds. It's true, but who wants to hum my stories to a pipefitter's tune? The poems have exploded from some subsoil growth on the rise there. And I end up with a handful of light-popped crayons. Why does this always short out in cupboarded poems, when all I wanted to do was orate in long strands my gemmy philosophy feelings? How did Shakespeare look when he wrote, let me see his hand positions. Or did he waste motions. And was there a cat in the room to go quiet with him, barely apparent scratchings. More apt a dog? Did he keep stopping, and then did he pace? Or did he run it all off quick spontaneous as Kerouac says in a sluice. The muffin jars . . . I have to remember to listen slowly to my lines or pay the price of thinking them wrong.

The light's avenue must be meltless, or risk rouge damage definition in the bargain. Subheading: Spalls. Between the gates of writing it grows hard to see. That's when we start the jokes of the two-handed pens. And crane to see the brains begin. And loft the yellow anklet over the tarn, lots past to see. The imagination is brought, now I view. Enough tattered and I won't swoon, over anything pictured cabbages huge on officialdom tar fire walls of recence in persiflage. The guy has got his door open and now he whistles rarely. Radio thoughtless provide backup of bebop harmonica. But why not then the clarinet? The meat marvels are cloistering buckle by vernal buckle.

It was as if a mystery tale in which the detective finally arrives back knocking at the same door as on the first page with the whole story to solve all over again. Art, Every Day, The Enigma of Bildungsroman Wick. I think it all back to when in the middle I didn't know a novel could be done. I thought it lasted and I was right, but in patches. The top of the mountain mirrored in the snow of its neighbor. And everything comes pilfering, allaying, exacerbating down. On the floor of this morning is the world thorn again. And I could bring another light or I could think, which?

Still the world moves on Beethoven. But the moil reverberates in its lighted car. There is a conflux reflex, you have to make sanity about if not out of. Whereoff the time of this window missing? The optics of data are arrows are thieves! And the music listens, as the painting pictures. But the glances cancel in too much move. I awake believing I know the exact fiberboard location in the basement of racks wherein the impossible to classify jam-date LP may be located. Those guys never even met in life. Which is why dual piano sessions never work out.

It's a battle on the bridge for the cleft of the ship rocking out by all tissue spindle threat-lights encase you to harbor leaving thought. In as much as the paratroopers fall they mow the lawn. Then many tiny hats have fallen out the back of the radio residue of youth chorals. Belief though all an adolescence of fading lessons.

I live in Idaho. No, I live in Saint Paul. No, DerryWheat. No, a Placer Del Sol. Perhaps CleatRanch Western? Or a Marrywell, Delaware. Eventually the rosters fine down to Rhode Island, palace of brad arts and the costume brine resorts. Here I carefully casually placed each rock in its separation paperbox, thinking them all eggs. What did I know in peacefully grounded window with the sun going off the dog. Illimitable breakfastfood message packs. Whines behind the radiator. Lump seeded yard flats with vanilla. The car again had gone away on my poem. Once again wholly I was handed back, bright sun on nothing to do starring. Worry not, whatever of the past you've forgotten you have made up. Never go back to highschool, never recapped on fool stool. Evidently enough tests gone past. Lincoln Logs to Gabby Hayes. My trains went down the garbage, the cellar which is desire.

I have no reason having enough room today. It rhymed all small, versus the strain world. The pincers emerging from gelatin thingy horizons of a pall studied. Added to the end of my line am I scribbling dutifully. Kerouac thought he was the end of his, a river delta depositionally subsiding. I ring his name for all crawl time. Singer creams to the bandstand and lifts one lip to gramercy. Above you see the flute towers and the acicular budgings of an early Stan Kenton. He was thought to be as gaunt as he thought himself greeted, nodding through threatens of corrode-dome arrangements. No more of him but in the settling atomics of ode riffs. I focused one ring on one finger that night, flew the girl and avoided a fight. FlickCheck Towers, Forty-Nine.

Not only do the big bands not come back but do they even stack up? Resounding crannies of smack took the toll. Now take Kafka, he arose in the morning no matter the shape he was in. As long as his and my and everybody else's brain lives in darkness, you have trouble with the moment, call it flute or oboe. I sense an orange in the hands of a stranger to your life. Brief glimpse of cracking darkness in the dayfire. Andirons cored with onions. Litmus sheets in a tight glass vial robbed from lab hookies. A grail robber who only could come up with bread in nitred boxy loaves. This emerges near the beginning of the delve story.

I walked into the room, why won't that lay flat? I started my mouth to talking. See, that's the problem, interstitial ramifications within the outset. Each two words throats too deep. Forgettal is becoming a premium. We became desperate to find a place to make love in. And everyone heated us further by avoiding the issue. A snare is a delusion, said the fiend. We finally woke up to the hopefully temporary impossibility. There we were in bed with heads. There the thoughts deformed in the ease of anything coming up possible. Dali put down his pistol and walked to the screen, pointing, "Theeese is the Black Christ! And THEEEEESE is NAWTHEENK!!"

Or models of deuterium a heated delirium. The nacelle on a French aeroplane, bumping down the triste companionway. What did Franz Kline hold by all those char-broad hackings? Whatever it was, you lose it in color. The women each a veteran of the silver screen but in a pointed script they couldn't blend, each to her own angle of blouse over breast. The wing strut was iron. The paint stroke lost weight at the end and slumped to the floor. The words were not sufficiently wedded in time. The compartment was dry.

The unloading of the cars proceeded in a shipshape fashion. The men on the surface of the moon could find nothing, even lost purchase on their own names finally. Their faces became disturbing and they took to hiding from one another. At last the radio rested in static. Nothing seemingly had gone wrong. But you must expect a story to turn. They are still there and probably still alive, they brought along so much oxygen and food. One might hope that they have taken to writing poems.

The term "epic length" is a formation of noncommunicating closets. Reverberations change the scale. Proportions are storeable. And the mind go on to the ends of the world? Reading is a drag because you want to have finished it yourself. I once said I wanted to write a novel that would be here today. Amend that to read, written already three thousand years. No, I'd rather write it than read it. Or at least get to the point of not knowing whether I was writing or reading. Silliness in folderol? apparel? What was that Godard word? Dreadful? Betrayal? Forgetful? Tigress in Jeans, Redcap in Steam, SkiTrails on a Mountainside. This writing has succumbed to massed flinch.

I couldn't sleep, so I wrote . . . Someday You'll Be Sorry, said Louis Armstrong. And that's it, no big deal! Applause. Musicians. Scars on the belly of the Flying Boxcar. What I want now is smoke from my mouth to lie on the air like hair. See what happens? I do tell a story and right away I lose my grasp on the functions. The peak was heated on either side by a sun.

A sentence producing pronounced uneasiness. Smithson's compact mass in a dim passageway. Set loss of vagaries. Carbonate integers beneath the barks of oaks. Supersaturate sentences. All My Tomorrows. Punctuation seed. Super heros versus fading laggards. The scent in the snout of the shoe. And the reason I could never find a decent insect book turns out to be that there are always too many species to ever reach classification. The novel has arrived, please send the key.

II

THE DAY THE WORLD DREW ALL ITS sense from Burly, Washington. This is the dimness of rooms, all fly with insensate savagery. The gold coat of coal going down a grey day, all splashed heat off the glassed-in rim. The wire is attached to the both poles, it will not parry me long. I want to pound over horizons in a Bentley with the banana shakes. And make the English meet with the snake. Highway, all the tarp from Tampico to Trotter and Dare. Drain. The carbon comes out all under the film wheels. Now we'll start the Carbarn Stanzas.

The auto once lit drew off alone beneath its radio shelvings. I was there, with another girl, instead of the other one, the one with starling stanchion memory braids adingle in the blanch of greypikes. Indiana undergoing chickenwire transmission. We laced onward, far as Born Tree. And the lacks there in the form of cats abraded in the expectancy of larvae. I knew the post, whereof it smalls. And the wind drains of all true arrowing in the mauve of trucks, their winnowing partials of the side as you trend the dials. The hard case was match point at a houndstooth standpoint, mixture of gulls. Playing of radio whims on the fronds, bone axials of town. You grow there, we wheat right onward. And the salads we can imagine, busting beyond. This is the road to approximate when I drove.

You would think this would all long have been filtered out down into special hidden velocity proximal glands somewhere body. Non. The light still turns to the exact shade of a glass in curve. The blood plumes to exact pitch spit of highway a furthering. I go there, wiped past in salutary gazing. Road fields a kite. Homes roam in itch. The alarm poles back in your smither days. Bone a kilter and half out like a speeding light, kiss that ties. But I'm writing this in a glass to windward December. East, and a coat of talon.

Barely, but the lights up day is a looming racer. And I must slim far in fractious buckets to keep up with my own poems. Here a tracing of the extends beyond. So keep my handle on a tavern for the slants bite later. Guy says, Bet you can't drop that washer on the tome of Pound. Long as it's marbled, says I. We each reach for our Runyon compass. Silly, but don't forget the ridiculous holds the roof of laughter and laughter is a spine. Only in movement are we aerial of the race. That and in Lincoln Nebraska there's a dome contains all the autos, beckon and then some. Rash as orogeny. And just as skimped on, Plimpton. Better take a new case, and this time have it hard.

In roof were all the vents allow the plasma in. That and the tar-black ventilators, ventral spirals that gnash. Inward information. Charles Bronson hawking lemons. No one could imagine a naming so cold. Flair pens. Bronson's face broiled in close up closed like a rattlesnake once upon a time in the west. They dubbed in the harmonica, his name later. Guess whistlers went out with radio, Clint Eastwood in a vacuum. I used to think all the action in movies took place behind glass. Dawn whole weed heights back there. False histories of say America still snapping in a clear-sided room. That'll give you a hold on youth. Left during the kiss.

Lexington Moneymarker Truss, sniped full of darkling larval beetles . . . Turn off the radio and breathe out the poem yawnly read. Danger it'll debrain your head. Still got your front brain, cat on the porch licking nice. Then the borealis comes ungummed, slips down to a sailor hat breakfasts. The day I pulled the wheat melt on her. Salt was on the radio. But that was another taunt, another thought on you, stupid magazine.

Time thread by and the walls come dry and the tiny animals exit from the people house. They are threats. To the carillon ropes of stationary time. Facient and come true. The people gather in their wake, wrapping too-late presents in opening lines of dark verse. Do not worry, bended fellows, the caverns will open their snops. You will hear the rhythm on your smiles. Just so's you're happy awaiting on Rimbaud to return his skill on the blemish atlas. Such a clear sliced fire remembrance of dawn'll date you, clued-tongue waiters. Jittery trigger thumb's the true dance. And player-typewriter for acute lead poems, clog of a morning.

But then as ever on the true blind waves a book comes in. Reduce if you could ever stand the amounts, paper backs. And you read it and you think how could this ever be more porously done, a wondrous of a shoe of a volume. But then the writing of your mind has you think the better of it, wanders of a sentence down the furl high way. Find it does, the dream holds servings. Driving on a month a sentence and then a fractured tree. That he finds it a giving up, to gather with others and it *is*. Breaking off the lines so they don't die but the thought falls anyway. To reach the middle of time, one's own a burlap field of battle, the ticking of the register off to one side. Bulk side, family wide, couching off the futures. But drive, he said. Or drive. He said, look out. Starving off that middle ever since, an amounting since, never still, holding to what are they hardly ways. You need impose a brightness when you read a thought book. The volume skimps, the gnarls are not. The blinding gives its weight, and how grey would you drive when it's stealing wooden clubs. Firing pool of the mind's golf. And the word "brought" overall as a title.

He doesn't have me here, he lost me there. And again. The man walked up to the door and knocked. Seems that inside were the secrets, the paving stones of habits on the break. No. He knocks and hears nothing. The street is all that's left of the cars. No child, no falls. He waits, listening apparently to all the above in the place of expectation. The walls are aluminum flash with sun. A cat arrives finally, an unattached nosing of cry and eyes. Down the street just past a lamp is the deathmask of a man who should be dead but isn't, lives. So it's night. So the thought is to pick up the plot where the last light left it. The light left us. I left my mask. Shall he back down the stairs. So the door is slightly raised. Now it's grey and the man has no notion of the time. If only something else would move. Seems he is the only else now the cat has left. Ignorant of the mask, he leaves. And the street was covered with trees, so many years, then they flooded the valley.

In the cave. No. In the room the lights brightened as the pages turned. The last page so overexposed the secrets could never be revealed. A large black cat on the folio of Moby Dick. He puts his feet against the wall and pushes. Stuff. The laboratory fills with sauce. Now there is really nowhere to leave. The monster had clung to the steeple until the hornets shagged him down. Now he roams unavoidable. And the game with the glass locks continues to be played, and the book all about sextons, or is it sextants?, continues to show pink, or yellow, or anyway up well? This is the perfect landscape for color photos that come out looking black and white. This is the hoarding of an utterly restless stillness. This is the Palace of Syringe.

Then he thudded his feet right onto the white mice that had appeared through the plastic of the ceiling lighting. A Count Basie record was spinning, next to the copy of The Castle, seemingly made out of granite. Then there were three bottles, three identical bottles, placed round to catch the three drips, three off-center and irregular drips. No one was in the room. So I get to tell you about it, though not even my self had been there. The room teetered in a sort of light black flat. Faint points of light appeared now and then from the distance, only to be immediately extinguished. The single but unobserved light in the room was very bright but the walls were of a greyish fur which seemed to produce the unbroken murmur of millions of children's voices. The word "goose" occasionally indistinguishable from the tiny roar. I intend to tear off this sheet as soon as I am finished with it.

No one can tell a thing in so lighted a room. And a room without colors at that. How can one describe the living space that occurs between all the words of a language? The ceaselessness is entrancing. The bell ropes hang from the outside of the tower, the resultant friction of the ropes over the brick sides producing irresolute sharpings or flattings of the notes. This does not seem to disturb the villagers who are never once solitary enough to notice. Perhaps they are deaf and sing. Perhaps they knock wood as a covering background. But I do not intend to be much concerned with the enumerations of the Common. I do not even very well recall the look of my own face.

I don't know what time it is. I don't know what day it is. I don't know but a dog is barking. Perhaps a snake will rise from the pulp hole of a fallen trunk. Perhaps I have no business in wishing for the sun to do more than dry a faint few streaks through the all-day overcast. But I will sit here and write till the plot is secured, wan hope. In the canyon. No. In the incredibly plain flat field not a move. A foot-high iron tong with its top inch bent over flat protruded from the low weed cover. This was off to one side, if I may be allowed. I may continue to wait and to watch, even again and again after variously extended periods of shallow sleep. To still hear the dog, somewhere near, and to grapple in mind for the exact location of my forgotten compass. The writing to continue if the perhaps one day perfect mind can not. Who's that at the door? My daughter with her pack.

The world lights up at night, this is one thing I have noticed. Another is that people don't think of things. This is apparent from the particular cast of their eyes into empty corners of space. Now, see? They are thinking of the others. Humans are an unfastened species. If they did not allow for the constantly changing spaces between them they could not keep track of one another. One comes through the door and another locks it. One opens his mouth to speak, another has drawn his stare. Perhaps they are purely propelled by fine-grained misunderstandings of exactly how much space there is to be had on this world. Here you can see I am already beginning to draw up my report. For I must keep in mind the ones in charge.

There are the stories of those who have managed to lock themselves out. Distracted by a cat with larger ears than usual, or cheek adhered to the bark of a huge gum tree. One would never hear their reports. Those are the types who would spend all day in approaching you from across the room in herringbone tweeds. The possibility of a herringbone rug. Make a note of that, and its quotient of navigability. Perhaps the material is more attracted to itself than elsewhere. Perhaps I should shift pens, or failing that inks. The finer the line the more knowledgeable one could be of the source of light.

Today is the day the river was discovered. Or could it be an ocean portion? Evidence from the vantage of a doorway is at best partial. I should get my best and only suit cleaned, remove all traces of wood chips. One I knew spent his summers employed by his father shuffling behind the chipper along overly wooded roads munching on candied raisins. The boredom was considerable, he could not carry a tune, but the accumulated data on barely distinguishable species of brownish-grey moths considerable. Consider all the volumes that never reach press for a variety of avocational reasons. As a man he stepped up to the water cooler as easily divertable as any other man. He had become fascinated, if so highly colored a term, with the subsidence of sedimentation in water courses. This led to a series of broken employments in parallel with the pursuit of a certain sort of horror tale development by which men are led down into unusually deep crypts carrying phone lines in the earliest hours never to return. Here we leave him. But there is no one here but me.

To continue with the books presently covering my water table, an enumeration. The Charming of Sullivan. Barking Discs. The Assembly of the Thundering Herds. Diamond Ides. The Still of Bees. The Book of Short Pants. The Hyacinth Opener, by Woody Kenton. A Neck Mirror for Alp Raisins. Get on with you. We lived in a house, I remember that much. Go on. A splicing of electric cords to restart the tumblers. It was necessary thus to keep the hedges at a distance. There were many of them and many movies borrowing my time. I couldn't stand my clothes or I couldn't stand in my clothes, I can't recall which. All I know is that it was necessary to repel terminus, if only by an inch. Only in that way could life revolve. Things to read grew scarce.

But it's this insane listing of everything that keeps you from ever possessing anything. One would think you spent your life at sea. Why don't you shape up and try to effect an evening. Women would perhaps begin to ask you. Troublesome animals would flee. Employments would open. Fur would turn to dust in your abode you would gain so much sunlight. Don't you think music has its place in the apportionment of magnetic fields? Take up the mass as a hobby. Study the use of the car at the first on gradeless roads.

But I haven't enough ear, I keep circling back to these apparent simplicities. A slip of the pen and you have begun to draw. The feel of the pants to assure they be straightened as loosely as possible. I fear I have merely abandoned all these men at their knocks on different doorways. One enabling clue might be this painting by Picasso of a girl at her morning bath in a pan scaled so oddly it appears she is standing in a beertray on the table. The bed is a mound of pearl butter comforters. The couch is marked in a zebra's blood. She is someway hooked there and if she can not move nothing else there can.

I am mistaken, she is a statue for an advertising stunt. The men all begin to curl their palms to grasp the handles on the doors. That's at least something done, the rictus of the uncompleted gesture that leads. And there again is that house I adventure again and again in my dreams. I know where it is, it actually exists but I have never been inside it, never more than passed it by awake. It seems nothing more than a plain and unsurreptitious grey two-story house with a striped awning over its second-story porch in summers. Why does it belabor me with its nighttime auguries of perverse dentistry and sexual flub?

Nine hands round, they all tug at once and what? flies into the air. This world is certainly unstable of language, not to speak of deed. The entrance to the ground is not everywhere. Only the chosen few allowed to shun the light. I put up my hand to signal the passing, for the time, of these shuttered tales.

III

MORNING AND EVERYTHING IS LOOSE AGAIN, the pain and all these transient robbages. The teeth are clenched on an alley thought up to contain spare parts. The crisis will come as a lowering of the trees together with an increase in heat. Winter's onset is like that, a myriad of slight adjustments, where or here. The night remains a midst and the day the extremities. Knowledge coming more into conjunction with an approaching hopelessness. All bills are paid on this machine, the word-printer that wounds me. Someone holds that only the writing will be taken as truth, but I not only can't imagine that being true, I can't even imagine the truth being imagined.

He had left off clutching the door handle in his gloved hand. It was brazen of him, and brazen is a fire and metallic in one, but he had made to imagine, there being nothing left in his mind, the nature of the inner surface of the door. Perhaps it was all a glistening sheet of tiny crystals of a softness seemingly impossible in a substance so bright. Perhaps a borealis of colors weaved through it at the humours of those beings within, if there was anyone there at all, he had heard no sound. The outside of the door was certainly so typically wooden that he couldn't quite grasp it even when looking directly at it and closely stood. There didn't appear to be a stitch of paint in the whole town. He thought for a minute of those others like himself standing entranced before equal doors. He had been told that they existed, had their equal orders, even looked fairly like him, and that their actions would be simultaneous. But what, with any exactitude at all, *is* enough?

These are rumours at best grounds for further salad days. I can't blame you as you do keep stopping to puzzle. Over all of us is the same dome growing tighter by the hour. Perhaps the amount of our ceaseless voices will keep the final perimeter at bay? I don't know. I only have enough cigarettes to last another day. This lighter on the other hand is patented to last as long as you own your smokes. Paper is no problem since someone keeps bringing me more. How do they know the time? They are so prompt. Sometimes I refuse the writing in order to count the number of pages left. Sometimes I want to question them as to . . . But most of my time passes in reveries of the nerve. The sneak attack which it turns out was known in advance, how was that allowed to happen? Only knowledge itself allows, that is true. No it's not. Some events have no semblance at all in the mind. They strictly occur, vicious word. The animals certainly are thoughtless, and the unpainted walls. A world in which only alien things can be said to be housed. The contents of bodies remain a mystery, no matter what has been laid bare in moments of fear. I am often afraid to open my shoes. The pendulum I can only dimly see through the stained glass of the clock case, what accompanies it in its daily rounds? A vast treatise could be constructed on the aids to interiors.

There is little doubt that Giotto himself dreamed that an angel lifted up a portion of his house, if not the whole rest of the town, judging from the tilted tower in the distance. And that he slept from that time in a perfectly curved condition, pointing then like the arrow that once launched circles to kill you, plunging through your back in the years to come. Figure one, a use for the mirror. I sometimes feel that poems stay like tobacco juice in the universe, of no use to men but of the highest importance to all the rest. Tuba with sidecar. The man's firing mechanism jams and he seems to come apart before the eyes of the henchmen. Those who by this time can be counted on to bring their own outfits. Slide of tree toads.

Next the picture shows the final resting place of Buddha, a greenroom. Shakespeare sits down at the table and begins to write and as he writes he starts to hum until it becomes apparent that he is not Shakespeare at all but Saint Jerome the Cro-Magnon crawler and painter of the caves. Faint turquoise patches could be seen in the shifting cloudbed. An eyeless spider paused in his zeal. And the door to the bath is locked since everyone suspects that there might be something fearsome inside. Pluto.

Did you have a nice time? I am too restless to complete work on the Book of During. This morning to only have time enough for *this* morning. Perhaps I suffer from a slight touch of the petit mal. Perhaps asleep I form my snores into speech. But since I sleep alone with locked door, no one to hear or if so, faint. The filming light has lined the eyes of far better travelers than myself. Mesas for instance have appeared cut by much too small saws. Islands in the stream too small for cars, or the heavy crews needed to maintain them. The lights go out in Rinseless Palace. But what's to fill the time while time is out.

But the comparisons . . . Say, a man's packed interior to a door's hollowness . . . There's to be no evening of the score. In my sleep are all the things lined up that I am in the coming day to be bothered with. Is the criticality possible to a mass to be an expansion or a congealment? Will all the buildings once knocked upon be revealed on the day following the wreckage from the air to be each carved from a single block of wood? Has a small portion of each breath been retained hidden in the cells of the body. Will one's work be finished in time.

While there I was at least able to piss on granite, the ingrained agility of that, though all the climbs proved washouts. There is something of dark import in the passing of the nimble finger across the bridge of the nose. There's the story of the bill of lading drying slowly on the greenish sink, never to be finished. There's also the one of the dog in hand. Then there's the day I looked at all my books on their shelves and repeated to myself, Blind as I am the candles must be returned by those who borrowed them. Their spines glowed in density. The birches lit up at the sun a minute. The words of address are fading into clotted codes. My answer is blunt: No limit, one more time.

IV

You'd need a paring knife to free this room from its smoke, my god. On a grid, the throat's residua lining up in its periods. The sun is lost again for they say the day is down. And I am sprung at this desk by an elastic weld. No other life comes possible but the freedom of the throne. The throttled laughter in duty. The clothes to be hung on the frame at dawn. The words of mouth drunk in of a paleness, pale of steel. Contentment, as any other function of decomposition, never rests. Over the gate here a sign proclaims, Smoke as Hard as Possible.

Meanwhile the landing was progressing on schedule. Rockets in dampness, cold feet in firm brogans. The beach head would be taken chronometrically. A large green bottle packed with filaments in brine was hidden from the fire. Without the aid of this invention the attackers would be lost. It was handed constantly from the best hidden man to the next best hidden man, for only in circulation could its presence be fully brought to bear. Of course the men knew little of its operation but stood in awe of its promise of success. If a man were hit another would be on hand to catch the falling bottle before it smashed on the many cobbles embedded in the sand. The enemy, hidden many miles back from the beach in a line of dirt hills hurling their shells, knew of its existence, understood even less of its operation, but stood in fear of it. They hoped that by a blanket firing of all their explosives the bottle might be randomly put out of action. I wonder if the success or failure of this operation has been properly recorded in the war department annals.

And on Nob Hill the man goes from door to door asking the same question, each time phrased a bit differently. He does not really want to know the answer so amuses himself as best he can. Another man follows him with a metal detector and a dog on a length of adhesive tape. Further down the street two poets in knit caps hurry toward the bank in the valley. The little scene keeps repeating itself to the eventual satisfaction of the men who have brought this latest model computerized TypeMaster to my office in any case.

I told you not to concern yourself over the outcome of the conflict. There will be no outcome. The procedure will maintain itself until it is replaced by another less familiar and more complicated. The prime nature of the question is a repetition that, through saturation and standing wave duration, eventually results in statement. Next to the list was tacked a manuscript casting a fictional light on the origin of the square in a fictional light.

And the jumping clouds rake the land with sun rays. Everyone involved in the outermost ways has forgotten to care about the contents of the room. They walk about in a wind of their own deed. They are choosing clothes. They are talking of hard things to be taken lightly walking in the alleys between the movie houses. They seem to be taking a hand in the witness of trends. Billboards are ruled out and pyramidlike blocks, purpose to be determined later. The Vikings, no, the lichens are closing in. And the wind brightens over the brusk details.

This could be a waterfall, and this here a notch in the cover of an old leather book caught in close-up. This could be a partially familiar saying, if only the rest of the page were not torn. Hand me the flashlight. No, remain on your knees. The rock walls are deafening, the waters beyond are the deepest known. Then crawl through this passage complex hewn of fruit crates with a sure grasp. What you know is not diminished by the holding. On the contrary, only the firm brain is much obliged to silence. If only this boundless telling were to stop! Hand me the orange. Hand me a straw.

V

Once out of the far side of the volcano they encounter a quiet valley, the sun setting instantly in color. Devious notion turns for the time being over, I wonder what actually constitutes the other side of the same thing. In consequence of this never having been examined to the point of proof, our mere life seems a fly-by. A more exact set of gleans should perhaps be put into operation. But who can set the exact duration of witness. For only chance determines where one stops reflecting, as Kafka noticed.

White geese there. Shocking brightness and expressionlessness. They were too large and would not let us move. They seemed to require nothing of us but that we do nothing, and would hurt us with their huge orange bills if we did not stay still. This was only too apparent in the blinding sunlight. No, you see they didn't eat. There were rumours . . . They were said to run on charged seeds passed one to another. The one doing the passing merely stopped and the receiver took up the attention where the other had left off. But no one had actually watched one of them run down. They were all males. Their unconscionable largeness was their major feature. They were the lightest of horrors. So many factors of the weave to be unforeseen.

But we keep going on about ourselves. Are there connections? Are we not separates in a variously sounded space? Two circles with dots inside means intelligence. No reason. I don't think about humanity but about world. Not these little set pieces they keep heaping to us but a whole churned fabric. The gods are not game players. No one knows I'm writing this, but the very act momentary of putting these words here makes a difference. The tree fell and before anybody had the chance to say they heard it or not the fabric was altered. Rilke nods that it has been long since any connection between the language and the things it names. But look at it that we are the connection. The enigma is a vast one, that persons are mere function of the set abstraction at our backs and the boundless irreducible we face. To open the eyes is ever to suffer the knocks of language unawares. Inevitably to prefer sleep to trees.

Yet the morning opens with a rainbow, where there should not be one, in the dry. The kind of event we see only to be repeated by itself. The knockless, but not lockless?, wanderings of light through air. And not call on the beasts to witness. But the sentence marks its own error. Wanderings performed only by the humans, and the neighboring wondering. The sky gone dim again, the mind held back a space.

And so at the last he became a painter of landscapes. No matter that he had spent his life mainly in pursuit of creatures. Perhaps he had stood in front of himself long enough finally to see things in such shape. The path from the tile set floor of the kitchen to the cement floor of the studio in all storms and lights and back again his own ground, the flame of his own spine set out in the world. I have all this time trod on my self, he said, and shied the next stroke through the wall. Now the creatures kept watch, through their holes.

This thought is a suck of broken lines. And, finishing fingers, I don't reach out for the plans to the city. The world is snowing, the trees so clear, the roofs diminished. Now no one to walk to the fade of walks, the loss of bodily parts. The painter drops a stitch, an entirely new set of pictures. That the plans not of the wall but through it, the table set up like a roof. Seeing is a march on consumables. See how in thought now the paragraph to shorten. But never that it's all so.

I was thinking about the morning and I was thinking about the rest of the day. And I was thinking about the rest of the day. Writing is impossible, the words are all there. Attention to a word and it veers you off any thought. Thought, the words have changed. Night as a function of width. Looseness as ample as your pride. The words advance to a thoughtlessness velocity void. I wish I could dirty them as one can paint. Meanwhile the circumferent thoughts to a central world. The time is up, since the bricks are being taken down. And straight lines get born because liquids stop eventually.

I don't want to speak from this place anymore. Rather a moon. Or a labyrinth of concrete cubicals once had been part of an A-bomb test. Green edge of a movie river, edge of a silent sea. The *backyard* of my head? The words are too typed. I hear too much heating system. I end up possessed by my own possessor, language my transformer. What kind of wind here to score my agency, scarify my stand. Let the mice exit the rock, it will be admitted. But if it's a voice I lead with then that needs to carve. And so far the blade is not finite. Hooligans wrestling on a mesa, under the slur of the moon.

The plot would be prehensile barbells. Or the man who attached his fingers to his wife's nipple for the rest of their days. For belief is useless at the razor, the hailing quotation of mind's lining. The way everyone goes away and leaves him lapsed into his own poems. I like the one that rocks, the one with teeth. I see the one I would write given up to silence various. Next we will visit the sun.

VI

THE MICE LEAVE THE BOX, CONTINUING in a straight line. For sure they don't love the world. Pencil in answers at the bottom of each step, fade into again flat clay. We don't ask of the world anything left. Stung brains worshipping straightness practice. The musician lives for his shot at impassioned linear continuance. The sense of Every Day meaning not a passing second without the fire of it. The verse of everyday meeting, the log of a dance. But does the jerk bump cakes. The lights open on the water, valves of the harbor. Animate strains of night flat. The days slow in the palm of the mind. The hair itches the day long. I saw the mice remove a watch from the drawer, a concerted fact. Bow to the furling world.

> "to make gestures and long harangues"
> to divest oneself of strong meringues
> to lay the cliff on which it hangs
> and bind the ghosts dilemmas lift

The mice are insects and walk that way, strict legged. They answer the call of the flashlight, line up along its beam. But I keep on shifting its direction, switching on and off, laying my own pattern. Safe, it will not bother them to stand for a chaos.

Chaos Narrows, Chaos Jumbles . . . What was the name of that vista spot? The slags of all time can be bounded by a map, the beings then tread oblivious. Let them wander in scarifying bands, fitting tin hats for danger. In time enough they will approach the pole. As I will never approach that window again. A kind of off-black ink at the lip of the page. Then the horror lurks at any opening? Perish the crossings.

I don't want to leave the mind's desk, but must escape the rule of mind's thumb. The supersonic plane reached its apex at such a height a whole range of distant clustered galaxies formerly unknown became visible. The pilot had not even pushed the special button, in fact, he had not even known which button to push. The one with the cap of blue felt. But the earth moves closer to other more impossible objects in our sleep. Bottles of crabbed sauce glued to the inside. The cat leaving tongue furrows in the butter left out on the counter. That huffy roaring of the air blower through the heat ducts, I'd rather were the sound of the clouds braising the sky. Or, the days when the clouds *are* the sky, was it O'Hara who said, Sometimes the sun doesn't set sometimes it just disappears. At the bottom of the year, right, the ills lurk, though they should be isolated in the cold? There should be and are alternates for every increment of speech, what a mad foul that would make up of the social. Would it were that I had gone out, if only I could have made up my mind to. The ossified conditional of relations. Wills that line up over the days only to just stand there resistant. The sandstone arch stood at the edge like a lock bolt, one foot forward to air the day out in the sun. That I shot it for its evident possession there, I now own. Ragged line of blue at the top will do for sky. But what made up the weight of it I left and left. The fortune of the other read: You will tread the soil of different countries.

But the man who wanted every thing in his home always in its place. The fly locked to the page, the cat to the table, etc. He considered buying actual tiny locks for the smallest things: brads or even motes of dust. Or Celia's thought of a beach where every grain of sand would come in its very own can, each to be opened before you even could lie there. Just another world heavy with intention. Hello to the man in the frictionfree suit. Alright, I do want to hear about it. Was or was not the beachhead achieved, and if not why not and if so how? At any rate, what became of the peculiar greenish bottle?

I am distracted by the neatness of the scatter. It really was the glacier, and not the "mountain-high tide", that produced the boulder train. Cataclysms are enclosed, sometimes to the point of invisibility, by the general all-over slowness of thing. If I can keep it continually wound the ticking of the clock will jar it over seventy-eight weeks to a position blocking my view of the Giotto. Then will I rage at the boundless ponderousness. The whole division seemed to come into view all at once, each member tugging his boots through the knee-high ocean. Any motion once started will come to be battered against.

Melville's Arrowhead, the second story so divided by a broad stairwell at the front, a narrow windowless corridor behind: his side, her side. That he sat writing at his table facing away from her, facing north, facing that window frame of Greylock, the double humped mountain white all winter lit with the sun behind him. That sun evidently hers and, as he said in a late poem, certainly Spring. The Winter of the Great Beast. The winter of my self come to get me. The putting of the head beneath the edge of the boulder and willing it to smash me, the balance being temporary anyway. Then the lights come on in the roof of the world and the writing continues under the whiteness of fingers. A willness of wonders. A shadeless contribution to the blurt of the art. The gallery an alleyway all crumpled in laughter.

Foghorn wants in here, and in addition wants the word versimilitude attached. But something scratches me, same root as verse?, so I check in the dictionary. Turns out it's verisimilitude, very. At home with the wrong root, all these years. Or one of those words that hang around, you even use without knowing the meaning of, having always been meaning to look up, and when you do. Wonderful when they turn out the opposite of all thought. As if love shared its birth with loaf.

The trees have been added to in sleep. Curious regional inches. Curts of bark. Escarpment swells. I didn't notice, I was being watched. Seems when I'm most myself I can't see. Bee seen to see, each at its time. Beyond the place of all seeing, a dream. Or the brass band I live in. The literature is tenacious but dull. You wander off among the stands in docile tremens. It is a Fourth of July with fireworks but by mistake at noon washing out the effects. You eat a rootbeer stick and tamp the ground of the former sparrows. A man is approaching with a hoop of a gelatin green. Turns out everyone is carrying objects they know not what to do with. Put them down or having done that with a fear of encroachment sit on them. The day whirls around in its picnic oranges and plastered ribbons as I find myself back on the lip of the orchestral parapet filled with a sudden inexplicable desire to orate. I fill my lungs and divest my brains of so many saved-up crossed-up messages, postage to the winds. But my band carries on and no one hears. The day goes down to silence finally, bland winds through soft leaves tucked in tiny lights. Graduation day of Charles Ives.

It's punk, that's all. Just punk, I think. The bald darts of occasions missed. A dreary world without coincidence. The whole of it stings without points of landing. Avoiding the dentist you'll be hurt anyway, conjuring fully the room and the pain. The lights occult in a two-minute egg, and the close enough movers of world push lame smiles. I could be wearing a pinstripe suit of gauze for all that attaches. The street is late today, and the ones who were to see to it far away. A giant billboard of barbell bicycle invention has replaced the natural store. Proximity machinery standing to repeat itself. The fade sun is an onion on a bridge. I confront myself and command.

He had no thought of what would come up, only the snow was falling. It was his own fault that he had left himself to live in a house whose only doors would open. There was a large grape on the plain or wall burning with a barium glare. Beyond was all women in coldcream raincoats milling in a skating fashion. Try to get a lock on this. All the windows in the city simultaneous, timed to the breathing of the light. The sun should be so lucky. Sheet glass on noiseless tracks. Pedestrians on shuttling rubber bands. Scoring by Harry "The Clasper" Barrage.

VII

LIGHTS ARE DARTING DEEP BENEATH THE WIDE open but barely functioning eye. These score marks upon the page the man is holding up in the darkness which when a finger is run across them will produce sounds approximating those of stars singe-ing their ways across the firmament. For thought there is no containment, it billows across every barricade, even to the dead of days. I know not what to say, what to hear nor see.

From the back wall of the narrow dressingroom you see her drape herself with gem cloth under bright bulbs then slip quick through the thin wings directly into the stage to do her number in even hotter light then out the far side away through tight corridor straight to a party slot where she raises a long stem crystal in toast to all gathered there in one continuous glide away to thinnest distance as if an icicle shot lengthwise through a blade-edge defile. This is a single even slice through matter from the near portion in which she is prepared to the place, open at one side for viewing, in which she performs, to a far extension in which the gathering is waiting for her presence to strike just the correct note of function and focus the whole tapering vista for one steadfast lingering gaze. Do we live here in the dark to all terminus or doubt the continuance of all sight.

The blade falls but the eye has seen it and sights the trace of its slice. Eyes touching brains at the wetness of their procedures. The woman has vanished, goes the announcement so baffling to the multitudes.

Then I see the horn through the snow. It is light and a cobra that rises, its skin vegetative but its movements all metal. A crystal sponge staving the air, the brim of houses and the lowering of the sea reach. I watch out and spin from my fingers the opal pendant, most vegetable of the mineral realms. Decay eater, bulb tincture of corruption itself, a gem fungus whose blaze is the tracing of foxfire. Vapour beacon of the woman's humours when pressed to the quick of the throat. See, she is ailing, the opal a mist. Triumphant and the fractures beat with blood. I have given mineral law to all sexual display.

But all my dreams are color as the caves again furl on beyond the ceaseless drenching wall. They pick up again at the god tone of the flattened stone. It calls without cease approachless since all the words are there. Each sheet transparent to the further's beat, a wetness to prevail on reception's ache. A point is always reached. Doubts in tireless process of sharpening themselves. But the sentence never ends. Whatever moons and suns and the laps of material filing that scratch in passing. The bumping of the wind on night's restless grade. Though the dream makes a loggia of Fields' stacked porches and a gift of the toy complexities there, only a tissue of the covering lecture survives on waking: "Your crystallized piss . . ."

And still the pieces of dust flake down, that go away when summer comes. The same falls of ash that enclosing him inspired Bach to compose according to the axes of certain crystal groupings in matrix. He retained a boy to bring them from secret vugs, you leave your hammer at the opening and that's your respected claim marker, in the Alps. And don't you know those topcoats are not renewable. But the thing once born gets stuck in larger and larger frames. What I had to learn was that the forms are happening inside the lines, not at the breaks. And anyway you know that keeping to exact line breaks, even to the point of always adhering to reading them aloud with that stop, is a sure way to go crazy. You break it just before the energy starts to drop, as Dorn pointed out. That's the only principle I know. "Your piss a crystal of . . ."

And what of this, half conscious, a continuation or a thumblike slurring bar? The asshole, not being so discreet, hooks to the bread at the end of the nose. This is a living in the unpoled world. And we will be short at the verge of the glaciers. Careful to step *over* the bergschrund and not fall down in and get extruded out the foot of the ice centuries hence, as an old glaciology prof used to tell it and cackle, true to some dear dead alpenstocker pipesmoker in the years before the lab took your best years. Landforms are fine, but that liverish sticklike covering . . .?

Grey south towns of New England in the smell, hoistings of chickenwire weights, stumped in the pall of January bearers, I can't but celluview and smear on by 'em. Same as before Creeley broke his bike up north: floor-pecking time. Like, what's up in Wilbraham or Monson, odd domed hills? Not a chance. Making ice cream out on smooth green lawns. They'd have to ankle me to the radiator. Commit Sky King on my breakfast daze. Off to scowl school and buckle your shoe horn, dreaming on the atrocities of tiger-eye weight freaks. I know your ma hove on by milk at the open window, under threat, all of us, of unsweetened KoolAid. Then the cows catch fire and camouflage duty's a mess. A washout, like Dairy School or diary lessons fast in the thicket delves.

The wall lay up against the avenue so long they broke down and bronzed it there. I know, I got let out to help 'em with the mumps. They stitched the cars to the mossy backing and let it fell be. I had to run home. I had to see my face in the glass, night plaque, above the neat note biological crenulations I kept in a sand box. This boy was wistful. This boy's wear was a tad striped. This could be remnants of old enough story or frame on what's left of the mill towns. Boulder train stone mill facade openings turned into Mill Outlets selling over and under alls in bins, fluorescent hand outs under the tube lighting. Once I bought a boiler suit there and lammed off to tear it on the coral hooks of those joint control systems soil west of Albany. Gleaming frustrations of intentions all down the line. Mosquitoes trapped in colored water bottles raised above the sink on a lark. Got out, stripped down, bloody mindedness in solitary gleans. Canvas covered station wagon in grocery crated field 'neath the Spelean Dipper. I put on the boiler suit and bounce down under the distance.

But the story loses definition in reminiscence. Cauliflower crusting on the niter-damp ledge, strains in solace under crawl stars. All the bridgings I got home. Something. But the stories once abbreviated too much collide. And there be shortings out. Leading to a completely new set of objects? Affairs as irreducibles. Cutter tales coated in their prime. Then and there Bach writes on shirt cardboards? But the knowledge on the door could not be read in an ink the equal of the wood. He had thought that only if the door could be sprung the knowledge would be gained, not knowing that it was exactly the standing of that door was the point. The door that is never to be opened enters the mind.

I don't wish to stand before the world and seek it,
I don't wish to twin myself blind.
Always turned to halve myself later,
wishing to solids the neat of the scatter
and cough up the time.
The world in such a twist to hauls all over again.
The mind half window half brine.
And all that is left a skitter
of meadow ash in the moon and on the palm.
The silence fire that gutters a bone.
The shorn mine.

The rush was toward the beach where the jellies formed into coins. The moon had left a ring around the strand. Jotting figures as of rusts in sand began to rhyme. And no one could stand on such a porch of brine heights, and no one could smile before the sun start its boil on the blade. Avenues shut toward all the salts and the headland veered from its resting vault. Shallows the dream and the time varies I want to knock back an inch, a blade off the duct sound desires. These are the spent ones, the ladderless reaches, the pint under a moon. We come to rest in the sandy corner of a cement stairway on the edge of a cliff, the cameras cogging shadows on the valley floor. Yet where comes the sun in this vertical world?

VIII

The blearier the men the more they stalked the black locomotive in the twilight. A parallel adventuring along backdrops of dull violet weed. They came to nothing, found out nothing, in the touchings of the outermost nerves of the brain to the dark shapes of the outside, shapes so dim they were filing themselves away. And the birds go up to the tops of the trees where no one will see them. As when sleep comes then the cat goes up and down. The links of all the branches threaten cracks to glow through from the other side of the fabric. And the men persist in their seek of the smudge locomotive. I have no further vision here except of men stumbling around a dim engine cellar in dirt pile dullness. All further endeavour strikes me plod. Tobacco light. He who is patient obtains . . . what? In certain cavern chambers I felt I was crawling inside a mind.

Under my life are the galleries of the circuit delves. And there is much there remains unravelled, if that word could come to mean unremembered. I walk forth on a thin shell surface I fear will increasingly crack through. My voice turns thin in the brevity of substance. I even fear to call. But so far I can still call it. And the smoke gains smile in its shelvings at the window sun. In all thus tensioned such murmurs are marbles, and the merest notion a rattle. Iced candle flamelets on the vanilla throttle. And there grows another mouth further down on the neck, through to the throat. It must become possible to speak with the lower animals through that one. Out in the slow light of the glacial top the day all the platinum stakes disappeared. With the sense that they had gone inward, behind the surface of all solidity. As in the silent dream I climbed down the abyss behind the radio in trying to fix it.

I come not to bad but to sorry. Nevertheless this all has a kind of linchpin severity. Swedenborg spoke of "correspondences", but perhaps this could be taken further and in another direction than that of the stratum of mystical glues. You write to friends and receive certain objects in return. These are then placed under glass in the collection hut or cabin high on the Schneealp. Returning to view and handle them again each summer the composer of bare intervals unburdened himself of the central coiled whisps of provocativity and at last arrived on the shoulder of lyric heat land. Here one summer I myself noticed a small ice cube that seemed to have fallen a long distance through a darkening shaft into the light of benchmark buds and drift wheat. Below planed the slow glacier, the one that had inspired Baudelaire to a coronal of IOUs. At the precise rate of thought these are the ordinary events. I picked up a pin in the sun, it couldn't wait.

I tried to watch that on a tube in the room. The thing? Oh, I saw that on the lathe of heaven. Did you . . . Did you mind? The circuit clicks off leaving the only motion to a pair of squirrels picking at the pie-plate covers over old pipe holes. The resultant heatlessness will not necessarily depress one. For the sun is out and the wind on things, the hairs on a bowler's head. Makes me speculate on the fur growing in the moist dark at the backs of paintings or even sculptures pushed back against walls. When I walk in the streets I see meters everywhere. I have not the change I fear. I hold not the risk of knocking here or there. I hear a ticking, always of other objects besides clocks. Must be their molecules are disarrayed at certain angles of the sun. Where is the man who will clasp to himself an icicle at the bottom of the year? I have often thought to take the time to watch things growing solid.

Grows itchy, grows straight away. Behind the barn lay an algaed green sump, whence rose the polished toads with veering eyes, thus the reference to "powdered frogs' legs" on the radio the following morning. But by that time no one alive within hearing, the end to another briefly far fetched story. The seeds developed unto death even before anyone could ascertain their existence. Thus does science develop ingrown hitches. The glass of water is always taken away before anyone is finished drinking from it. The album played through with a lead rod. The green flash beyond belief or exposure. The pin at the bottom of the pot. I have told you and told you.

Then the lights came on again, shortly but briefly, and the groaning hefters groped for their clothing and an equally ill-fitting consciousness. The barracks room was painted in a vegetable but nonetheless blinding Tahquitz orange. Perhaps the intention had been thereby to burst the men awake, however cratelike that notion. At any rate a line formed leading creakily from washroom to entryway to a dimlit outside standing around. They await. They attempt to read the type on their shoes. They watch the sunball rise behind a clanging rustiness. They see the treed squirrels eyeing them from variously acrobatic angles. They wonder just what is the work for them *this* day. Will it be more wheat to be aligned or a whelming despair at the ledge-sized fragments of iron to be whipped from the dells into place at the perimeter of the campgrounds so new to them. They had arrived over a numberless succession of nights entirely spent hurtling through tunnels, a veritable decalibration of the compass. Work was after all everywhere to be done and on time. Teeth had each to be tuned by a fork proper to only it, and cabinets of a greenish porcelain installed on every pole by the way. Gallons of wire had arrived at the camp, a sort of violet liquid that achieves tensile lengths when exposed to the least puff of air. There were these tasks and always more to be done, none of whose eventual functioning they would ever witness, for by the time the final adjustments, always made by others in their wake, had been made, they were always already on the move elsewhere. They were commonly known only as The Spiders.

And in the restaurant, a noise. The glass top of a medicine bottle, salt, had fallen against the chromium molding at the base of the counter. A slightest pause, following which the patrons ate on. The radio had been removed, since the uninterrupted talking thereon had been felt to constitute a confusion of the conversations amongst the eaters themselves. Thus the unfolding of the species proceeds further into self-containment. We will no longer admit to the possession of outsides. What's to fear? There is nothing out there. Meanwhile the diner, cradled in cables, was being lowered gently to a spot on the tundra by helicopter. Standing room only, for further thoughts on this matter. Emblems of personality will not be returned. The cruciform piece from the base of the stem continues to be kicked from foot to foot at random.

Then came again the animals. The aloof snort snail, strumming his glass ear rods to good effect as tweezers. Through the agency of this one, odors could be perceived purely visually. He disappears down the carbon lane, as if a gruff rug were tucked at the edge of town. Next comes a lion whose torso is composed of a trembling peach bag, from which bellows a report like audible parsnips. He is erased at the edge of a weed space by a passing glazier hefting his sign. On the three hinged panels are shown: an oval pile, seen as from above, of assorted dark greenish substances thought to represent a theory of magnetism; a bald man in shiny black uniform with a sawblade, toothed on each edge, in the form of the Xtian symbol for fish depending from his horizontal left arm; and furthest to the right, in fact pushed right up against the border as if by a great but invisible force, the pink palm of a human hand on which has been scattered an arrangement of thistle seeds, to all appearances the metallic punctuations for sentences of words which have vanished. Now comes a flight of pinpoint-sized beings able to raise and lower the surrounding temperature by varying the frequency of their buzzing. These seem drawn to the point of a distant peak whence they are heard to disappear with the sound of a large angel cake dropped to the pavement. Then the lime worms, borrowed from the neighboring town, short themselves into the ground at any point, eking out a labyrinth of passageways of complex extent but such narrowness as to prevent human investigation. Knowing these worms to be tireless in their excavations, and so fearing the collapse of the very earth beneath their feet, the remaining animals hiding in the wings, and there are some fascinating examples such as the Zeppelin Spaniel or the Cleat Hog, have announced their unconditional refusal to appear here on this day. Thus comes to its end yet another world.

IX

I MUST TELL YOU THAT IN ITS ENTIRETY I cannot fill in the landscape of my own background. Great gulfs exist that I can plumb exactly with resonant pendula but cannot describe. Even the letters comprising my name seem to me divided by such gaps, each one at variance with the rest in its extent. Too, each letter is sounded differently, as if by different instruments, making up a klangfarbenmelodie. Each one of my works attempts to reproduce this nominal effect, but seen in such a glaring light they all must be taken as failures. Perhaps at the last I myself will more perfectly come to resemble my name.

I look around the room and see the pieces of wood that perform their functions of holding up my frayings. The spaces between them come to light and I walk there among armatures. What shines more brilliantly than dogged failure in the annals of coincidence? To smoke a cigar in the darkened hallway, to be shot by a nervous cook. And still the bare intervals will chime in the crystal light of the slow glaciers. There are prayers beacon prisms at the thin places.

I am a guard of the law and come in at the door to find the floor strewn in a myriad of salts, the residue of countless candle-flames of utter glance in the solitude. Left to me it is all done excepting me. I must now go forth unerringly to the still point. In the balance, the heart stone, the mind strand. In the mill pond the currents occult a shorn diamond.

I became fascinated with precisely where things were missing in the world. Actions after all leave gaps to ponder, the slightest empty crack as the place where something happened. If it were a movie they were making, everything possible would be taken away. These rocks were filmed. That swath of cement. Those chairs. No, not that one, these over here. Then they were taken away. Now they are here. Since that time some of my hairs have come loose. Others have stayed. You want to be the master of what you say and do, you want to be the boss of tooth decay. You want to shoot horses far from their stable. You must delay the filming of the film.

They made it look as if the building was another building behind the building far removed. They made the cousin be your brother. They brought plants in, then wet them. They licked lips. To them "hiring" was a part of chemical procedure. They thought all you had to do was have a certain face, particular from any angle. Speech was a transferable bonus. Light from the sun was now preferable not because it *was* light from the sun but because it made everything look as though it were lit by the sun. Later people would say, this is the place where that film was made, only somehow it looked different then. No one and nothing to recover from being observed.

You imagine yourself driven to walk on the perfect lawn of a becoming familiar town to speak words and perform gestures perfectly unfamiliar to you. You stand and turn between picturesque buildings and try not to think but to gain purchase on a fragmentary identity someone has just handed to you. This is your profession. And then to be taken away in further cars. You are revolving on pole of numbness, flecked with too many colors and signs. What you say could as well be what she says, it says you will say. A man standing next to you worries only about a possible loss of light. Another is concerned with the randomness of unemployed persons. But what you are all involved in is the construction of a grand interference pattern, one of your stray thoughts.

The light comes on now in the hidden calcium, now in a framed patch of weeds or seats. Get a tight shot of the man's hand just as it is about to grasp the knob. Approach the wall with a neutral intensity of focus, as if all the world were a periphery. They saw themselves. Yes, they saw the selves. They saw the layers of stocking before the shelves. They saw the hands that had moved before they could see the hand that was there. They preferred the overlay but were always prevented by the present thing. What was present always blocked the view.

Airships were leaving the gloved hand. Glue crystallizing between cement blocks. Opposite ends of sentences wrapping around stalking legs as they faded. And the only search worthwhile was the underlying one for the repository.

"Good afternoon, Mister Blanding. And how have you found your flight?"

X

THE KHAKI PLASTIC SOLDIERS HAD BEEN PLACED on a green plasticene board molded into two facing ridges with a river of blue poster paint between. Sentences of description tend to loss of kilter. A few of the model men had had their legs cut off so that they appeared to be standing hip-deep in the water. This comprised a project that my daughter had been assigned to make for school. The teacher had decided the time had come to fill time with a battle. There seemed to be no other rationale. An evening had been spent in silly contemplation of plastic men's postures. The time had dried.

Outside a snow had finally come to weigh the bare board January. The two articles could exchange positions without disturbing the balance of that sentence. In that way a perfect equation is assured, as with a tuning fork. I have no problem with that. I'll leave as planned for Nantucket by night. The file drawer was shut on the spilled can of coffee or tobacco. No meaning is perfect.

The question of night had come up. Night had arrived with certainty. The lock on the lay of the land was secure. There was no limit to the manners in which the land could be laid out. A cough was heard from the upper left dormer window. In the town car in a word the function of moth-free bats was the topic. At evening most of the constituents tended to be silent. What is needed in words? What is mated in other words?

XI

THAT SQUIRREL IS HOLDING AND MUNCHING on an orange section of my this morning pancakes. He's staring in at me the while but I'm the one wondering about him. State of the world is a froggy hibernated air, cold finger joints quail. Then as if the air all turned into a single light translucent and floaty kind of vegetable. As I wrote that down the squirrel took advantage of that precise moment to vanish. How much I do owe to one Philip Whalen Esq. of Oregon, Kyoto and San Francisco.

Durer's angel still disturbs by his stare. He wonders if this section of the universe at the least was created by him and if it can now be turned to some use. After all, fol-de-rol. A world of measure bolts and slotted leathers, no squirrel up a tree.

Cold fingers, strafey mind. The trouble be, there's no iron in the wine, no wire in the tree, the colloidals have all come bumbling and combing down. The larch could be turned to litmus, the acorn to tea. Long live Anna Livia Plurabelle.

In this portion of the world there was no mind. Boulders all took up the time. What plants there were flinched. The sun beat time and the colors ranged. An off-color range, one might say. Nothing to do today but disturb in inchy eons. One would search in vain for the least of eyes. Clean sweep in waterless situ (where did I leave the brads?). Normalcy turning grey over the view. But no eyes to see what I here give you. You being readers who have long since lost hold on the rocky terrains. Wake and sigh, weep and ache. This world has lost its last wasp. This world has not the chance of display in a lemon-glass window. No scratched frames in the Film of Vain Design. Boulders have the say and are not, or take too long in grainy dispatch. Observer gone away. Rhyme pick its teeth. The Soldiers of Saturn agree, elbow down on bended knee.

They builded great cities and read them out of the script. Hooks and crannies of stone deserted, read back into whisk rock tome. Aisles of salted and crack-dome budgeless, the writers have formed away. Short day at Standing Creek. A typewriter out of millet seed. Haul voice down staircase of canyon dense. The warm down waters wormed away. The voice to work in hinge and cease. Vast pillar pellet of a crow. Schisty carburetor of a cow. Brain out of sod, bulk, drone. There's no fiddling with flattery, no function to the cone. We have allowed ourselves the elegance of voided pages. The horn no longer sirens at the pitch of the waste. Dry lake the home of a minor being.

But at the same time in another part of this same world, a guy is washing his hands by an artifical fire. At the porcelain sink he feels himself to be as pale as wax and imagines that he hears his washing hands echoed back from the mirror opposite. Soon his day will begin, as soon as he imagines it to, as soon as he hears the outside roar of trucks and cars start. What is the agenda.

A veritable armada of things to be done, all in tried and true time. He pats on his pasteboard suit and bounds down the stairs humming a tune about bears dreaming in hibernation. The sun beams down on wet pavements as there had been rain in the night, he thinks it so, as neatly awkward as is managed in prose. Will he go to the zoo or to the factory or to watch the fire that has been burning in the lot down the avenue for days. Are there as many choices as there are words to tell of them. He walks forward as he thinks to himself. Telephone poles and barber poles and poles holding signs up to see, the poles holding traffic signals and lighted instructions. There is too much blinking blankly world. There are not enough animals today. There is a dog. There went a cat. There are people no one knows. Stories of finishing and waiting and plots. Once he had wanted to go fishing but the waters withdrew and the fishing stopped. One could wait until something happened to one, out in the middle of the starey street until big earthquake stroked California. There be movie houses showing turns of old rope, and shops releasing the odor of clams. Purveyors waiting for their buyers endlessly. To my mind these people are all too much the same, he thought, every face like another in the past. He would have to go to the zoo, there to view the smart black snakes and the hunched gorillas hiding their lunch. He would rest on a bench by the termite dwell and hum all his tunes to the pitch of their buzz. Insects after all make the finest of backgrounds. He would be on the watch for the solitary white ant, its call like a coin in a pop bottle shaken.

He must have slept by the hives. His dream the colored eyes of iron buoys blinking in the swell of a deep sea night. Accompanied by the smell of shuffling feet. Oranges would taste good in the low sun of the late afternoon it now was. He toyed one out of the last vendor fading away. A lion's yawn behind the penguin stands. No one to meet, no one to share, no one to join away the nightful of rains. Not even a bucket brigade for the chance and the fun of it. He walked down the cement shafts of the elbowing stairwells behind the rodent labyrinth. Darkness reminded him of stories, too many of them spoken all at once. He flushed them up the flue of his mind on the breath of a single lamp point at the end of the dank corridor leading to the street. Now it would be time to dwell on precisely nothing until tomorrow's light.

I just don't know. I don't think there's much point in keeping on breaking things apart so you can see their shiny sides. Aren't there enough edges of things sparkling in the world as it is? You could keep running around feeling them and thinking on them to your heart's content and still never exhaust anything but yourself in the process. There must be space enough for the light and sound to come through, don't you understand that? Yes, but so much?

I know what we'll do, read books to eachother for the rest of our lives. We could do worse, I suppose, we could go out and bother other people all the time. We could make food, lay it all out evenly and then leave it and go out to a restaurant where we could grow angry and send everything back to the kitchen. What about the movies? Agh, who cares about those hairy old braided things. There's a raccoon tail right there on the floor in front of the television set and the big window. Yes, and half a glass of water left over from last night, but I won't say just where it is. See if you can find it. Later we can have an argument over the first man to climb the Eiffel Tower after it was completed and then water the marigolds again. You're not paying attention. To you, or to the wind from the sun?

There was a cool breeze off the water and she wondered if it was that that made these red itchy blotchy places come out on the backs of her fingers. She reached for another Winston. If men had breasts they wouldn't put their cigarettes in their shirt pockets so casually. The low sun winkled the boats that bobbed up against the floats. She wondered again what was taking him so long and began to listen to the conversation of her next table neighbors. Something about the price of salt in Afghanistan and whether that had any affect on the price of the rugs they were considering buying as an investment. The prism in the harbor light lit up and began to revolve. They said the current in the channel was too strong, unswimmable, especially at night with the mako sharks that came nosing in from the open sea. Nobody could imagine themselves to be in a position to do more than have another drink and see.

What's true is that the world is beyond the mind. That and I have a live shotgun shell hidden at the back of a letterfile drawer. When the clouds burn through a little orange, then you know it will not snow more seriously. This cigarette smells like the inside of an old draft physical summons. The other day I had my temperature and blood pressure taken, both arms, and they were normal for "here in the office". No doctor knows more about my body than I do. They seem to know all about "the" body, under certain conditions and the influence of certain texts. A slight error and you have a new book about caftans, or capstans, or the graceful rudiments of Jo Jones that led to the finished four-square procedures of Max Roach. The sky seems to work alright without gears and with just a touch of iris agate. When you love someone you want to *be* them, to live inside their bodies and speak from there. No doubt the world would lose its pitch without the infinite gestures of juncture your thighs compose.

XII

But then the world grew rude as rouge on a honeydew melon. Great grace notes of abcess rose from the inner shell. You have no stitch of knowledge that isn't based at the thin places. Lineups of stewing pomegranates trace a grid of magnetic phosphors on the ground. At a certain juncture somebody rises. Speaks: None shall pass the fixed features on the statues of limitation. Full stop. Only then shall the fastened world prove luminous at last. And the suns roll away to the furthest boiling blacknesses of fascination.

Or is it termination? In sets. Rows of stalled cars, batteries leaking, eggs in their sandwiches. Then knowledge is only cast shards of a certain fascination. Light pours off them at once in every direction. We are blinded and conceived. This is written in a hopeless time, overlain with darting sounds, which once to grasp them would at least stir up the mix again. One just don't know the results of yet another stir. Out at the pumphouse gather the men today with wires in their heads. They are trying to unravel and order the jury-rigged systems. Every thing come up with makes a layering on others past.The everpresent notion of an overwhelming cause again puts them off the scent. Begins to appear they are separate problems. Separation Grouper. Or whatever common hidden as ever. Each eye lights up a singular shaft. What I heard said turned out untrue. The united untied. And vent off rage. Stand around in the air too cold for smoking fingers. Talk of waters that have got stuck. History is with us, a celluloid billfold or a squirrel investigating the pane of glass. Put things together and watch them shift, drop out the holes between thoughts. Notional stealth insured. Animals without backbones are not supposed to be pressurized.

The Devil? Who knows what that might be. There must be space in the Grand Design for beings of great power. Contact with them would never be direct. Incantations on odd domed hills? How silly one would feel with the dipper on its tail all alone. February and hatred of frosted hemp lines boarded to the face of the month I was born. Loose clattering things in the darkness of soundless winds. That you tried to stray over there and back between dateless trees, traceless of witness. The night is no cover, the stars are apart, their sparkle a pickle of the air-bloated eye. Far storms on a sun, twitching of hair trigger a Japanese camera, brandnames computerized the Song of Rice. I am hied away in a car of air. Is time a fluid of meterless finitude? The love I have spoken is desperate enough. Clouds of plugged source filling the mines of earth. Hairs on the paper my own.

Think of all the things that are wrong. They make up a crystal frame for the target. Blue sky patch where your or any face enough might come to be. Outside is all blacked off and mute, the lights and sounds far back in my head. Courage then is the focused beam to the beat of the heart? I rose in the morning and thought askance at the lacquered tasks. Once and again, laggard tanks? The row is heavy to heave and bites at the knuckles. The light is impatient today and the dropped boat makes a blundering ring. The ears grow a furze of coffee overblown with cream. A night was spent with the chattering ducks, unspun, not facient. The plods are still on the wall in pales of spunk yellow. Once I saw castle rides of jeweled circus there. Once I was an Eskimo in lava. Once I had uncapped my pen at last.

The haunted house stayed locked. It was easy enough to imagine what went on inside, even in daytime. Something from outside had shaken it once and matters within had never again quite settled. Its inner spaces seemed filled with a dark gelatin capable of time's slow motion keeping things suspended in undulant swirls. A place where nothing had ever wholly passed. Small girls peeked in at the black windows in sunshine and glimpsed their mirrored inner faces tighten and gaggled away chilled. Tales grew out of the hovering vacuum.

The house was a noun. And if you spoke close enough, not with lips but in an olden center of mind, you suddenly as if always knew all that it contained. Numberless things and beings of voice and motion, now you could hold them all, as in a teacup silverpoint crumb. All language history and universe held in one coined bolt, the first mark shied on the wall of that cave where our species first learned its responsibility. The same mark that had first struck the knell of time.

The Mark of Outside was on the land. And we would be crushed by space which gains mass as time dissolves. The proof being in our learning to forget. First we would notice that language itself was beginning to baffle us. Overload of terms as a gross message dawning in the mind. We are being pushed out. Thought itself condensed beyond belief. Considered world succumbing to a heavying paleness of mind. And the white whale sprung back, an occluded sky, too close to grasp too vast. Just time enough left for a final pass of the well worn "too late".

XIII

I WONDER ABOUT THINGS AND THE PEOPLE between us. The currents, the feedback, and the whelms. The sharp cracks between trees, and the tolling between the knees. The world is sharp, narrows, and perhaps lost. But I was born on an avenue, though perhaps too short for the name. Now I skip the yard plots and end up in these wood lots. Do you wish me to tell plots, to pronounce names. A walk in the woods would last a while longer than some of its beings. They die loose since they never came up with time. Step over by and around and sometimes on the small things being a history of this world. Shout, as you're shutting the book on the roles.

Nobody has said to me Stop when it mattered. And I go on doing what I had been doing in a manner that keeps its lights trimmed. Push the finger into the woman at the point of lash control. As in sleep we lose lives in ourselves. Time to matter. Time to cancel the fly-over. Time to fur the wand. Is there time for control of the slowest, as we know there might be in the fast. From which we speak we are hidden, as the lines of the walls have the parallel power of candles. I lie down abed and imagine your body in all its positions at once. This is a speech from which, as in gnarl of chemicals, an act will proceed. Time seems insistent on the singular. If not mere alone one is next.

The woman rises, her breasts never the same. A man's wife's body is the greatest mystery. Each time it is revealed. Do you know me? Each glimpse a start, each stare another. And the removal of tight silks is a peeling away of skin to expose the more sensitive flesh beneath. What was your name before you were born? I wish that only I will know it. Standing unclothed across the room you are sensitive only to my eye. And when I cross to you and enter you I will infuse you with my sources. A kiss of my extremity speaks with you inside. Then is the world shut down for awhile.

The world is coming up to us all the time. It has its chicken and lands. I see a greatness in dull whacks, light boards and snooze. The buckle on one's carapace, who can assemble it? Pirates have stormed the land from the north down to the cove. The new lights on your itching wrists are the sealed product of rice. A nova occured at the black rim and brought them. There will be a ruby soon, it will be the robber of dense.

I have no call to say this but I think you should store my place. Needles are required and a shut solution of darkness. The chickens will chime then and the warts on a pickle rise adroit. You have no sun here but often a moon, it curdles the wicks that singe dreams. And the constant drawing toward and away limns a hotness. The man stands on his own hands in the backwards, a land of longness and told gaps. Buzzings in the nose the toes and the penis. Lights that at night are holes in pitch, turning you each center whichway. Each one writes a novel which is a stream at the bottom of the yards behind the houses. In the way that no one can hold in the mind what is constantly on the move. And the hero will be kneeling in the turns on his mind. He will be the Borealis of the Wheatrows in brown corduroys.

XIV

But i want to trace myself clear of the spots I have faced. It's nine below zero in Tobacco, Ontario, just five fenced pull-ups from the Dew Line. Leave the door open when you leave and an orange moon. But it's incapable, this bruised, or is it burnished?, Standard of Excellence, fog world. Stomping down the leave trail home in yellow heavy boots. But I thought all it was I was coming to a cave, hidden shack for a door down. The world is not brought back from a trembling portion nearby. Interdicts. A rainy grey pencil day, barely adequate. Now it's all trotted out in sun and frees waves loose. Think out a water to walk on . . . Didn't you loose?

The road dangles past the avenue blocks and fountains. I could write a million pages of subject with no answers. And in time rip the whole thing up and start again in kneeling silence, taps in back of battle cans. It's not the con that interests me but the bent, the laugh forms that come from stint collapse. The reading of Thomas Wolfe behind Indiana dunes produces what furtherant fixative? I stood and washed Chicago on the lake of all salt thought, wrote letters home in duty of romance, crossed a rattle track in rains and strove to avenue my life on. The radio always in nearing eaves was shot with a burnt sodium, billboard slant at a roadcut, righthand teas jarring in the rail dock. Where staunch on? And is writing to fall from highway fingers by a sea? Scribing inward always plotless sea? What stocks taken inheld unnoticed at the time but determinant? Then I see that when I'm stuck for plot I question, and questions are a cycling back to refire the opening? I could fill notebooks with a wide howing power. But I should sketch more?, and stanchion the puzzles in my wake. I should learn all over again to hand-write and steady the verve. I should slip off the path oftener and nod like bird in full peck. This basement is rancid. I should investigate turrets in a momentary risen, investigate pipe sections in glows of inward day under the ramp post fixup shops. I should come down the stairs, with copy of Big Sur surprised, surprising title, 1962 in the hardcover, $4.50. Stand out holding on but not yet reading amazed.

No car go by but asks no stop but in going tunes the route. We could be down in Newport on a lark, a rock by the sea displays. We could sandwich talk on the mountains noontimes. Talk over music, how does it last, how does Monk pause. Now I muse away from the music, missing its hardness. I can't grasp it anymore, and if I dig down too far for the crystals I will strike the gym floor. What does prose and the cat relate. There is a severance of titillation in the later years, an addiction to honor one's own character. Am I coming back to being the hero I one time thought to seem? Books are weightless, but plots weigh a lot. I lived above a yard once and buried my laundry. I have the poems to prove it.

But the sun's a sinker and the coffee was cold. I'm a waver, not a buyer. What if I never stopped but drove on in a Cadillac wishfulness west, parting all the stoves and the titles for buttes. I'd wrest a cigarette out of the sun's grasp and music would rise keen to me from the stinging grill. There's no rest in the game of inches. Thinking on all the tableland around my dreams of town. The latches to are only dreams. Stop fingering the writing and drill it! String back home on a hunch in your head and stymy past thought to allow, as if back were out. But I sink at the typer and the world skids out before my paws. Style's all a matter of rates.

And the man walks along the many too many times sized-up street, he thinks beans, values, the wire grill along below cornices wrenched loose in a storm, and what if he followed the stairs found to the exact angle, would rarity arrive at him? He has left his wife nude in a furnished room and wonders. The lint clothes draped on soap racks could be construed back to what fleet sex scenes in sealed garbanzo bulb cells broadcast nights. Meanwhile how the clouds poke slow as cauliflower through the hem of a wish, leaf. And the ivory nodes idle up the avenue, clocked to the brim in levelers of day. He has his thoughts, those stand-ins for pauses. He contemplates cares taken with the ends of evenings, when the siren's on and the stories float smoking. He enters a padded entry and slips lightly on the interim disappearing.

XV

THE GREEN SOLDIERS STILL WISH FOR A LOCK on the vanished bottle. Where did it slide when the battle was a hill in their way? And who keeps it now, as what trace, in knobless cellars? The night came quickly, silence, and the absence on a rain. They encounter a road in the plotless, and thoughts turned backwards. The bottle become a dream hum of stakes at last won. The suspicion was rife, it had made off with their lives.

Now the museum now the ledges of apothecary stalls. As the man is still stumped, stubbed before his door. The witnesses are reduced to what spins in rows, untied and on shelves. The candle stubs at the end of the age of writing. Volumes that are vials and fill, on axes of your turning away from them nights. As if pauses of thought were increments of brass. As the shades of drawn battles are out shining the bees. This is the kicked-in section of the Village Stales. But I want it to be colored around the edges, stained actually, as with blood. Or ink, since it's seemed to me that blood and ink are of the same consistency. And then the coffin is put on over the head as if it were a lace cloak. And then a tremble comes from within as if to suggest that a breeze were stirring. Around the back of all this is a waist-high ledge soaked in the wax of a century's dead candles.

I coughed and the shortnesses of night baffled me. Because I have always known that everytime out is starting again. I delivered myself backwards into the hands of the ghost. Because I have found that the reverse of life is an awkwardness of beauty. The world is tattled around the edges, and the purities come humbling down. Hatred is aglow in the farming sheens of the bypass. We go, they say, and the heart is adjusted. In other words parted from carelessness. What is seen from the back of the car, continuous and vacuuming away, is the seamless acuity to death. The highway is a perfect undressing of luck. The highway has left us with lucidity.

But it is obvious that the man has understood nothing. It is obvious that the man stood around waiting. Cocteau tells us that the chain of current events may break the thread of the past which once was the best investment for spiritual funds. What does not quote dies. Nothing passes but a toted solvency, read as totaled. Maybe the whole is but a protein mix? Last night the ghosts rented a hall downroom from mine and settled the game of forgettal. But I have misplaced their memory, their moves.

I must read and I must smoke, I must lie and I must die. Dealing with the shock shortages of my remedies, high voltage intransigence. I would deal in Mozarts, but he is just a kid. Nothing is more marvelous than a clock that has stopped, the ring around a hole through which water pushes. When I write a line I leave the ceiling alone, I time the knots in the breakup of clouds, I master the flinch that parries the flocked hollow of timidity. The moon has come out when a sun should be. So be it, so a stop along this fear. The lights are riddled in ons and offs. The black is our solvent temper. Then a battle scene is my love story, a tenderness of fault blocks.

Give back the world, and in giving back the shadows that steal across the sky. My world is a bird forever locked in light above a chimney of the twilight. This figure a prism pendulum stroking the dark of a nervegrain poetry, starting point, stoking that. The light is on, the earth is troweled. The eternal remains, waves gone with light. Turn from the lair of the cold wicks. The half-life of bone awaits. The public throat is a klaxon breeding wa-wa. I think back to an avenue of a size I once took. An avenue is thought. An avenue is width more than length. An avenue is thorough. A street is long as the next life. The avenue is fronted with stalled things. A sentence grows to a point. The heart is a walk and the eyes that bar it. I think therefore. I think peter. I think then all this the night brings to a wash.

The Joy of Learning is a film of the smoke curls above my cigarette thoughts. It moves by the static that states collision. Island sounds are seconds or models for them. The radio stripes about the void. Great to teach the enemy that he says to know. The substitute of some small zero out of the necessary. The world is composed of orange rinds and bicycle lamps, the world that is not composed as those things are. I live in composition. In other words, confusion, will, and doubt.

We do not understand each other when the record interferes. We side with walks which might take us beyond thoughts a flicker of chance sets. The cigarette on the edge of the world, a scratch of paper on the surface of the blocked hum of words yet to sound. A flatter where the book is bound. But I don't understand where my self is here in this coggéd heat. I suffer from the small in my largeness and must stripe the ants across the rugs. Detail is aboil and lies in wait for me. I dream of an Italy unknown in black lacquer boats and oldness. I want to move in great flashing strides across the blocks I myself have built out into struck crystal strew of shouting eyes. What is the point of it, where is the point of not saying things?

Cut glass flowers, pencils and bark. Lamps that are stone lamps and speak night. Fruits of trellis band and hands that will diamond-tooth and slice them. Light berating horns, brand boots that poise snails beneath the walk. These are the stalks of the play that chatters taking place in a rubber emptiness. Will anything I have finished stay proud enough to nurture this? Will madness be stayed by the one hand raised and the other weighed down in object? I have a time, I have a time with it. And I don't think I wanted to know. I didn't think it was possible.

I want to tell the story that holds in wait. I am held by the hand that in never quite touching the handle reminds us of how many times that door has been opened, so many times we have forgotten what lies within, so fixed are we by that opening and shutting the contents of our very memories have become a mystery. The hand passing and passing over the candle flame, the other hand releasing the damp closed green of the battle's bottle.

XVI

It's the history of wax is the history of us, our knowledge. The history of breathing that drops on the page, no matter our strung intentions. The history of intestines along the road of stone forts. We are told these are stone walls placed by hand, but the way the vines close to cover them we know the story of blood has dried here.

I trace my steps from the shore and back, from my desk to the wall. I nod up against reaches that tire me. The logs stalk across the boulevard of chalk, and windows dim me grievous and slender. The battle is from the brain outwards, why has the jelly innard boil not grinned through the bark of the trunk? Because my thought-muted gaze has stamped it. And thus from here must proceed the Mystery of Holds.

What are the rules? Metal plates of a thinness over the parts, that a pierce might come from within or without any guarding of the hindrance. Who will trouble the skin to vex over its contents. Only the voice shows subscription of the hidden. The hand that catches the skin in climbing the pure rock sheets. I grasp on to the interior of my own body. Own pain given voice, given hidden pleasure, smoked out of hollows on the trek to the shining and thus blocked cove of divulge. Inside are the horrors that the brainy have placed there, hoping for a chair to their closing residence. A sentence is the apt to find comforts of a closure. In penetrating the bottle in thought he perpetrated it. Lank coincidence on the braided hand. The face was the enclosure and voided his thoughts. Only the voices of infection are hidden. The walls stay rampant. The flags have concealed the insect sunset. But it was the crystal in terms of work that blooded the victory.

It's the history of war as the history of sex, the waiting for a hashed-out plumper knowledge. We believe in the cone and we train it to hold our water. Five specimen days. And a satisfaction more slaking than the bottle it came from. In Shakespeare the glow cannot be reversed and we stay with the music to the lasting of the first mark. Da Capo, El Capitan.

I've arrived at the want of nothing further, so await the stopping of even my waiting and holding further. These paragraphs stay the hopelessness of blocks. The door holds the skin from its innards. This is the history of its errors. But the story you wish already is in its cells. An unraveling of the body in the twentieth century, a quitclaim descendant of continuance ridge. A bee's eye view of Emily Dickinson as she puts away always her things in drawers. The writing will be snubbed, however dangled, we know this from the start, any flinging down an avenue of dwindled but speeding starts. There was so much to do that no one had the time to find the proper drugs for its use. And no one could hold to any further concept of noon. The world halted in a boil became a current image on a stamp. But the letters would continue to drain the confidence in time. Failing the hand on the right beast.

I locked that door from the start, it's my watch and worry that you follow here and start at. You overstress the empathy of your walls with mine. They shored up in waters so further the vein was overdone. Read the book, stop the flow, tap the keys of the machine on your knees. The flyaway is a combine of all the booted errors. The screen drew blank and the shufflers lifted. The bank had been conquered but not the face. The expression drew features of errors from its trace. Perhaps I live in a piled brace. Perhaps I dawn on one.

The men walked past the lifters and out up the headwall of the camp. They had the time for one last expression of soon empty duty. They had washed all the doors and now the time had spilled over the brim to leave. But I keep finding ahead of myself. I keep leaving the completion before the next one is missed. Is this very thought and what fell does it say. The walls had hindered the approach the kept mind maintained. It's the keep going up there that burns away your mind. It's the subscription mind we keep stealing to gain a march on. And the doors turn solid sooner than we know.

XVII

HERE I WILL SAY IT, but it keeps leaving me. Here I will parry with elbow of monk. Here I will return from the moon, but there's a catch to any catch of light. Holds that revolve 'round the spineless mind as the straps fall from the body of dreams nights. There's a yellow patina on the plastered leg that wasn't shown before. Liars are we all so bodied to our constituency, of a reduced gold the moon stained a pillar for our hollowed young love. And where I had wedgewood it had better said wormwood, the flavors of a drowntable blackstar abutment on coils of essence and fingers tapping gall. The Latin is divided on this point.

How to say, wrung of all sky and mean it today on the prisms of inwardness. The boys approach the face of adventure but my words again saddle their stall. I don't know a thing but point. This must be the riddance or the absolute. Why am I shut to the present flavors? The knife calms down between a coin and its absence, that coin being my name and who would flee from it. None but my own. In a word mine my title, all riddance despite? And I see myself step up to that face, so thought as if handle ever gone.

From here on this page the world is unknown. Thus start enumerations of the hidden. Upon the layers of subsequent rock earth and seeds there lies a layer of birds. This data is taken as an active consumption, even of the earlier strata by the capstones of the sentence. To dissimulate is to return, as on the noted planet where at a certain age one turns aside, grows back through youth and finally has to "go back in". The birds have disappeared. Why then is there anything left visible on this descriptive world?

Why stop there? I have an urge to continue each sentence till there's no room for another, then the urge to stillness stops it. So I go my way, by myself. And the windows of the world click and the trees shut. What's name would bear repeating? At such a point words tear my thoughts to such a pretty pass. That Picasso's Egyptian lady covers the Delicate Arch. And my room fossilizes as I watch back to nineteen oh five.

Not to be entirely determined by the recently read. I have seen the cloth that sticks to certain shades of air. Tell the story that has never been thought on before. The one that raises its own hairs, volleys down its own passes. The mouth that opened in the box canyon asking for a halt to pastels. Mesas are a natural for the notion to bore holes in a tube and blow. As the jay hops to the branch, the tree slows down or slows it down. I must have a work where things go.

XVIII

But they have left me these things and what do I do with these, lives of another's. The room fills up dim with dials, lock strap equippage, plates of loathe trim and the encapsuling plotter clogged to the rugs. Give me strip knife, hand me load gash! I would have amber to the rub of peeling flesh, gone off tap of all seas in a hammer, raised as a code sun. But here these brag cliffs of fossil dispatch stuff brown as the passage of a lug. Duff cloak jointments in apparel lodge about to bulk in hedgements and bump. Barrage as a mountain will stump, no chance of stem. All an attic of brawn baggage coughed up into a seatment, dump poise, from which no shout ice is visible. Give me a ledge clocked off from this in sheers, blue day down and far. Not this balance fuzz for the moment cheese! For this I eye as fudge batters and my wrists will not cock. Where is the sheen sea in concatenated hall drawers? These clogs will mount to clatter slant full and where then short hand life? I fear a baggage mountain will coffin me. I light a cigar and hop, stung phlegm in place.

A stoutness budges hemming my outline, hand on a brown star. But the world is snaking around me, puffed at corners and slant rake. The black pen clicks itself on the pad and the desk. Things dance away from my touch, stir along the chasm of flatness reaches here to there. That I am tiny away in the room I am thankful when things stop full before any edge. They have their terrors too?, and I can sieve death from a long way off. It gathers to snap and pull the hair out by the threads. He passed me, I saw him, an ordinary stalker. Only his hat away spinning from the knife of a wall. No blur at the moment one's got.

The words are sorted out in snouts and plaques. Even some snake pods there that scent a heat through the clothing. The clapboards of the housing dotted with spikes of blood ram a vacuum through a shoe of nearing closing. All these contained in a bottle, held to be shaken in variously leveled moods. Thus and so is the world full of holds. The mystery's gone locking.

He has hired himself a place for the night and feels there are candles lit inside the walls. These shuttered flames will give him no peace and he is sleepless. Perhaps he should hire a cat as well to keep watch on these things no other man can see. Like a cat he can catch the hiss of the tiniest ignition.

Science terms burn in the refrigerator, which is a file drawer with the label "LOG". I go over there sometimes and idle under the fluorescents. I watch him work long hours on the work of importance he calls "papes", a tissue pile of nicknames without even benefit of coffee. What will turn out, niter tinctured cotton rats? I should finally tell the story of "Face to Face" and the whole long while walk up to that. Would it all take longer than my desk afternoons or should I take short shrift of type and balance beams with relearned pointed-up and perfect longhand? How long harden in the pretend of writing, till a wordless thing shut dry till nothing stirs? The world is coming to an avenue of my sharp place, a neatness to think so. Walked away spelling out over his shoulder, "I could fill barns". Knowledge is limitless but has its edges. And a plot could find a balance in incompleteness? How many nervous stares at harvest moons until barrel will roll to exact sight notch and lock? In this Ode to Incapacity I dare a day to accompany silence. When I have seen you means you're gone.

Waving hello, below the nut barn and just past the sample factory, where the wheat flake boxtops are soaked in veneer. I can't stay up with you, says the Medicine Man. I think perhaps the Great Light has gone Gaunt, and the hand so near to the knob of the door has fur on. Oh, for the farm fields where the simple lights will surely grow, and nobody lacks a halftrack balance of scouted happiness. The youth's earth height is a begging elbow, nurtured in cereal of a plum. The nose groans to peck in a hopeless dialysis. Shouts grow up over a bladed gentian. Dust bins where we could have hooked Shelley, all grown over in a braided dare. I could repeat things, I could tame myself, I could back off from hairs so untouched the sheets are still uncut. Nodding light at the end of the smokeless tube. Farming has dimmed from the celebrated arts.

Stipend for the needless, a newness all weighed out in stakes. While wide out sea washes yawn from sight, and a lash past Paris. I intend to and want to do it and I feel a bit foolish for not. But rather gash rude birds in the wall with a blade. No hindsight means no future will hold. New species of newt suckequipped for tapers of the space needle. I want novels of a page rooted well as flanks the heavy haul pants. I want grounded vitamins. I need to think sight. The prospector boots silver barrels out of his way to the gold.

XIX

Birds function as a leveler.
Brides function as leather.
Words that function only as I don't want them to a furtherance follow-up on that. The leather is a kiln, gingered with bridal plasm, a limestone hoodoo of the creaked backs frosted in lash ions will blow its whole rugged top half mast to tic ash over whole crystal counties, suspending cookery till the spasm flush. From the Book of Holstered Castles the whole House of Capacitance. How about that? I was, but did you listen? (come to be, come to be) I wonder if you ever saw me here, when my thoughts are on hold. Probably you never saw me elsewhere, the cranes fly. And at dawn I close my eyes, to the slice between earth and heart. But for the cruelty of arrangement they are the same. But for the cut of plot words merge. Everything I say is to windward, where the margins damage. That the mind turn jade.

Sorry about pitifulness. Sorry about lapse and spurn of the fond. Sorry I must make words do. But what further sigh would be more telling. And what is telling but a yearning true. A word as good as a hand to a blind tattler. What is the extent of the room for holding knowledge. How else could I come down here and say that the door up there was locked before I could get ready for it, walk in and say what I thought right to say. Just to imagine that the light in there was low, a diamond locked in amber catching the starshine. Nothing ever heard was worth preparing for this moment, the one of the larval watch termed heart.

Syzygy. Thought at which the wrist is shaken out loose. Discovery of the battery the bottle really was, under the elm load in the attic. The magnolia tree blooms against the bedroom of the discovery, the wall of the morning light. I think we fell faster after the touch of that delicate angle, the arch into the future of youth unstable. Like piling up cordwood to the limit the moment the buzz. The limit of light finally written on the window shade, the lampshade, the lid. Then I walked backwards till my childhood was hid.

The precious and prehensile fallacy is that the words *are* the world. And you. Captio omne. Want it and want it now, now meaning all. The whole friable world coming into description in possession of you, and the words would take the load, if not the lead. Know it that things are people in this, given their equal stands and slaking lozenges. See it that a tree holds more than a mistress on a thundrous whole afternoon. Hear it said in all its circuitry of vugs and catacombs the litany of the crystals, where Munch said we glow in departure of all earthen tones.

As information becomes more numerous, the distance between its facts increases. This is thought to be due to the fact that the universe, though infinite, is expanding. A fact is (something that is) made or done (facere: to make do). If they say this is not true I will make it be. Is the distance between minds expanding? He watches the dead spider at the base of the wall. At least we have room. Who is Balthus? And why did no one ever lean over against a table that might well be a piano in quite that extendible a way? The ones with potential are the ones that don't *lead to* anything. History being a blind in all its devices. I'm talking about the vastness of crevices connective. And I'm talking around the first word that will be surrounded by silence. That then finally to be infinitely listenable. Civilization as a closed labyrinth of approach roads . . .

But leastwhiles it's a home on the range. And the buffalo shards in sixes on the seismic kit. Puffing to weights on the ramp lamps. Forming sleets in border. But is the dormer the resident or the window he gave down from? You have to deplete your margin at edges. And closing on the horizon is the blood opal signet ring formation gadget of the Phantom Cart. Will level us away on plying our functions.

XX

TO MAKE A NEW BEGINNING ALWAYS at the close of the summer. And open the door and let in what, could keep on going. Could keep what all going on from coming back in reversed sizes. The transformations are not only animals, though they seem most easily to take that form. Take a farm in the sun, what results, or eventuates under moon? Who am I planning these plots and asking these questions of? Any arrangement demands of me an answer. A bog or hug at the dormer or door. A tug there. At the balcony depending on a sea. The picture of a door with hand shadow attendant but inoperative. It is a question. The handle is a witness to the dislocation, an inability to spring from object to answer. I disagree, or the door can not be opened. As if there were no way to use the phrase in a language. Stop me if you've heard this door is not there. Now it is *all* here, rustling like cabbages too closely affirmed. The answerable has no shadow.

The world is slow and ugly and pitted. And the face won't come out of its blare. There are things, but I won't say, enough to crowd me. Engines sounding in the night, seeming faulty. Where did I drop an elbow on the wrong table starting this fork? Why does the ceiling not raise a glow, start in to crack?

In the light this morning animals, or *are* birds animals? The Beckons, including trees. A stillness that, even in motion, does not wait. On what? Me. My arms have been oranged brown. Must have chanced to see some sun. Organ, of the lift in a room the music might make, or to pull the wheel of the car up. Flight, that is neither from nor to. A story that is held in its darting complexion. The troops come whistling up.

He wandered in from the hillside and touched the bottle in the window. The grass thickened in the wind behind him. The glass tightened in the mirror behind the window. I was not there. At any rate I could not have spoken these words.

For that matter. And then he started up at the window again. And then he started up at the window backwards. Had turned his back away from the street at the sense he was watched. The eyes do not possess this sense. Other tenses. The sentence had opened at a window opening, some speech on the street, eyes on the opposite wall. A man jerked from watching position into range of a mirror. The parenthesis that can never be closed.

The street moved out of parenthesis. In the mirror the window does not frame the mirror but the street. He could not help watching from the window that his speech would not loosen its form. In the window in the winter in the comments after dinner. The size of wall at which I do not greet the night but inch along after it sentencewise. In the milk of the speaker. In the glass of the plumber. The wise do not intend the casting of lengths. Then I rise, I speak, in the place of the former. The sentence is the longer, then complete.

Night time again but not in the telling. One would need a further chalk. I would need more than one to set upon me the trace of no light. No weight, and wind, and wheat, and violent drilling in the past mind of a violet cast. And will this need dream gumption? And will this exceed sleep speed? The lines have been pouched in this state, the lines have been pretended massing. The battalion passed beyond the hill during itch producing slight roll. The speaker does not wake. As in the mirror the close does not close.

I have not awakened to the avenue of a change in season. I do not pretend that the men have reached a farm. The telling will have to be lifted a bit before I go on with the story.

XXI

But does the story move out, as of a house to where. In the story he told he lived on the second floor. But narrative does not (easily?) possess an ascendancy. He wanted to walk down the street. He wished to walk backwards all of his further life and never be told of his act and to continue seeing the glaring world fleeing from his reach.

He walked backwards down the avenue with nothing on his mind. Never again would he worry past windows, conceive of any passing body a threatener. He could have been waltzing for all that passed him by. His reflection led him out of danger. Facades seemed to float in rhyme with the chunks of metal hurtling past on this calm afternoon. He had left it all behind, for the moment at least glorious in thoughtless but visible retreat.

The room had been left perfectly disassembled. Everything, as his wife revolved, nudely, slowly, in an untouched corner with a top hat. The bed legs sawed off and the mattress stuffing packed neatly behind the closet door. The wicker of the chairs unknotted and laid out in parallel strands on the floor. Everything of glass smashed and then hammered to a powder practically invisible now. But the windows had their frames removed and the plate glass carefully outheld to drop into the alley below. The food had been eaten, methodically with no regard for taste or hunger. All clothing sliced into swatches in the same pattern each time. The cutlery beaten into twisted balls of silver. Then, on the threshold, he wet one finger at his lips and traced in the air the line of the lower curves of her breasts as if he would take them too. Justice.

He was cool. His mind had tamed. No one could see him. He began to reorganize the city.

I want to leave these fixed words and enter the dagger cities. I want to go, see myself gone, off and still seeing what attaches to my last exiting lifted footstep. Encounter the platoon by chance in some backalley countryside, share a deciding card with them and break bottles down the long escarpments. Open the theater and let out the dogs. Enter the zoo and remain. Clip coupons in cellophane jungles and pester the vanishing species. Where are the Opium Wars and the cloth jut of their spangled tongs? I want to open up resonant naves in mudworld. Take a seat on shockwave bus. Gallop through the plates of chandelier hoards. Give myself thanks for the leaving it so long.

The ship will approach my retreat.

XXII

In the memory ward...

The story was replaced by a government report gathering all previous feelers . . .

Concentration was required, focal energies in a concrete bunker . . .

He sighted the lines on the desert floor, then blacked out according to so far unexplained causes.

The significance of dots in a straight line has so far gone unnoticed by the great majority of the American public.

It is possible to extend the fingertips beyond what previously . . .

Suddenly he realized that he had in fact glimpsed the trace in the bottom of the tub.

The day dawned crisp with line-of-sight to all horizons on a need-to-know basis.

How many and in exactly what proximity do you suppose it would take to . . .

The lines of all possible literatures brought together in a particle. And then some guy stumbles into the bar stepping on the ant. There's this problem of the "just about". The point really being that we wave away from it. The light on the ocean liner finally put out. I was a member of that band in the lounge. Huge imaginable caterpillars and a rose diamond high on the thigh. To think, one could exhaust the subject of Cold. Bring down the matter of Patience faster than Balthus. Put his head in the door, shout "Creed" and then remain standing there. I took a step beyond the land, I held what you would leave on that desert island in my hand. Telling up to wait, it is hard. I put on my bifocals and got over the food.

It was not hard to see that the spread of radio waves weighed heavily on the populace. The never very even tenor of the moment. The heart tips in balance with the particle. We don't know which way, we don't know how or why the way. He decides to show the world a movie of itself big not sad. But if you write you will find out just how long you have. Just as granite is withdrawing from the world's picture. I tend to lunch on sundays never other days. Then the report is placed away in the drawer which in shutting catches the dress of the tight young secretary as she turns to rise.

They were beautiful things for houses. Gilt brocade and solder ware of roofs, immense canopied beds with organ pipes for posts, clouds of opaline shell at the corners of walls, silent fiery fountains falling on black velvet. Buildings whose character shone only on the insides. I will take a walk and speak of wondrous things and never leave my house.

There in the hall were the pears, and there in a pinch were the stairs. I have no sense of making things two which is circumstance. Or is the Whale in the Jardiniere coincidence? Making up a reason or the time or a bed, we come to the last hall at the back, which is a chapter containing brightness. It is never darkening.

I'm teasing the tulips, she said.

To write a novel I would have to forget my own history.

XXIII

I SIT AT MY DESK AND DO NOT WORK. I lean back and spit into a small can placed for this purpose below and to the side of my desk. I do not do this, but I think about avoidance. I think about writing it down and I do it here.

All that to present one word, a token and the state will go away.

An alternative in so many words is the unnecessary words that take up what's space? They also have a stake in your future. A small can placed for this purpose below and to the side of my desk, etc. Description, the taking of a long time to finally push the object away. In this case it doesn't exist anyway. I am subject to my work: Power! To be the victim of the attention focused outward. At the university they were placed in pairs of seats so that whatever occured they would feel responsible for each other. If I fail then he may also, the next in turn. The light was extinguished and the rest of the lecture took place in darkness. Questions were always put in the most extreme brightness.

Raise an arm long enough and you will receive the pain of its settling. Well, as they say, if you behave yourself, then you are well behaved. The weight that is felt behind the eys in certain hypnagogic states. The root of behaviour?

The word "purpose" inhabits the same mental space as the word "future".

The small can that does not exist . . . or did not. Now it does. I should examine it further, look at it closer. It has a bright red tomato painted on it in a circle of white. Surrounding this in a kind of frieze or wreath are green leaves that look more like spinach. It is small enough that it would extremely difficult to hit with the spit. I have the unsettling feeling that I did not invent this object. It was there, appeared to me at that precise moment of syntax, merely to be described. Discovery of another sort of vacuum that must be filled? The very figure, for that moment, of the word "avoidance" which had taken that route to come into my mind. Understand a-void as a-moral etc., to be *not* void? The humming circuits of the complex . . .

The continual questioning has become a deep unease at whatever is put down. We now see too far beneath the surfaces, without a thought, without even meaning to. The I's behind each I, you, or it. An ice piano that has exploded through the walls. Things that may be understood better as events, they exist for so short a time. The handwriting dissolving under the pressure of rates. Does it matter that a connection is not made? Perhaps that is to be preferred?

On the map, on the wall, the hand left a triangular shadow. Here is where the army must be. Now here. Now here. Then it must move to there. The pins that were stolen from the private's shirt: he should not miss them for he would be dead. He will not miss them for he shall be dead. The platoon had been moving through the forest on Operation PinDrop. Then the unforeseen mines had frozen them in the mud of their tracks. The general frowned and baked his hand over the brandy fire. How did it go?, the novel in which guys go and things come so it all amounts up to a dare and a date.

Then Philip said, the stalactites felt such an urge to come into contact with each other that they filled every surface with a prickle of tiny points. Millions of men in a room scratching and shouting at eachother. They do not agree that the situation truly is as it has just been described. The surface would come apart otherwise, bringing down accusations and hands full of a glassy ham. The concert could not proceed, the wires had been removed, the listeners stitched to their seats. On the stage all that could be seen was a pair of wings, like harps constructed of moldy satin from an old sofa.

The American Public is unknown. They have their work somewhere off in a math-green room. How could one take one's cues from them, by doing always the opposite as Cocteau in his time could, when they know nothing of us and care less? The battle plan had become a slippery stack of transparencies. Everywhere one looked the deep lines of the dots, the zeroing eyes, the viral bearings.

XXIV

And dawn never broke this frame of my concentration. The angel seemed to want me to stop, not to confess or consider further, but merely stop. This is the reason these words do not appear in my Diary. And I began to realize my memories as a shuffle of still pictures. Postcards they seemed to be, The Dream of Innocent III for instance. And I saw this as the true state of things, a timeless evidence of incidences. The time before or after an event is lost and in fact never did exist. The building crooked in its raise, no otherwise. Is it then only an extreme shallowness of consciousness that gives us this continual sensation of transience? Now the light of full mid day comes blasting in on me through the big window and this is all nonsense. But still, that author, the one that "has described this landscape for all time"?

It's a shock, the realization that nobody knows.

But that tap of the hand which seems to breach that gap born of the knob, I attempt to rinse my mind of all but what furthers it. It is the business of doors to seal, when they stand open then rushes in the mystery. As it is the function of the conscious to forget. I learned this once behind a friend's garage searching beneath wet leaves and a length of chickenwire for a soup can filled with photographs cut from a magazine, postures of the nude body of Diane Webber.

The end. Could be. Then the book would be only a statue worth its salt. I see a glow of landings, blue with starch white towers. Pillars under the sea that glow an unspecified orange. They will never find things there. The boats do not arrive. I do not see any beings there, though maybe they are smaller still than my handwriting in grammar school which the teacher marked down ("If you do not use my microscope I will refuse to think your system markable.") This all exists on the third planet in the Logorrheic System, its sun a star of the vast dim red type. Too obvious to be used as a target, too monumental for any schedule. Its inhabitants, if any, lack the characteristics of communication. Pale vistas of solitary tools.

She lay rubber on the sand. Behind a screen . . . No. I could reach her gaze only through the lens between her thighs. Those prong toes kept her tendons taut, spelling out the words in the sand: OPEN TO FEAR. It seemed that I would have to miss my appointment at Key Largo.

Those black eyes on the fence that jolted me so out of my childhood home shoes. Black eggs that required bone shoes. I sped home beneath the heaving leaves' black undersides. Why did Surrealism reject music, because it was an invention of writers? Would a Surrealism of musicians have rejected sex?

I know nothing more here.

XXV

WHEN I CAN NOT THINK OF THE WORDS, the words do not avail themselves of me. I look out of the window and see a windward tree. I sometimes think the words are beings who absent themselves, as why should they not have puzzles of their own to trace. Then am I locked in a mine and the words are leagues beyond that wall-face, or banister, Roger Bannister tiny in the distance and running away. Do you ever think anything of Freud's methods?

I take down a sandwich and read it but do not eat it in the morning. Then the klaxon sounds. It is the radioactive waste vessels ricocheting between poles and treetrunks at the sleeping driver truck wreck just down the valley. My dreams take me to large events concealed in fine exchanges. The horn between the teeth on paper but wearily regarded. Then toss away, then in my way, then doggedly hitting the highway. I don't understand, I champ to occupy the precise space.

There had been that point in Chinatown at which he interrupted nothing more important (a love scene develops) with the remark, What's that in your eye? She, It's a flaw in the iris (pupil?), a kind of birthmark. Now what did Jack Nicholson say then? And did he next move further west, his lips to her lips? And why does this appear, and just what? There are certain screen partners, large as the screen can make them, large enough to occupy the narrowest of one's own possible beds. Cancellations of the reasons a reverie might thus be struck. Calls attention to a point heavier than fire to the gaze.

The point is that a sticky substance might form on the bookmark between the pages pressed to make an unreadable but (therefore?) comprehensible solid block. He fears. He nears the dip of his finding days. They take the picture of the day on bleachers before the cave. And following the impression they descended. A point of sparkle in the eye an amazingly exact turquoise. Her later career would be either one of liaison with a rock star or a whoring on the Golden Coast. Or perhaps death in an open car, the one eye blown out. I put this down in my note pad. Typed it would enter a book. Slipping into form of a fact, inflected thus neglected.

Imposition of a tape he would stall. The subject was of two mouths, but afforded no entrance or exit. The answer was thought at the time to be radio. For you they will continue to follow the story of the Pine Hills Toucher. He lets himself in to the screen-damaged room only to find her next-to-nude body sprawled in the contents of the open refrigerator. A reach for the wall-phone indicating police in the background, the plot having once again come to turn upon itself and the yawning of the typing watcher. Once you get him in there how does he get you out? Snatched venetian blinds of a further southern California. Lightning storms apparent at ends of all the darker landings. Once a voice now ticking in the loosening spool.

The words that have been damaged in the nooks and crannies of this filing country, America.

XXVI

THE ATTRACTIVE IMAGE is an attractive hazard. Remain attentive on the lip of the thoroughfare. That they landed in the jungle capital and put up a goof pad. And the jar become a bowl to be contemplated in the feedback fastnesses of charge night. Then came a knocking at the door. Behind the hand was the American Friend, pulsing for a scraggy end to this terminus.

I tried to look up, to look it up, but the page always covers the page. The girl walks on with a red notebook, she thinks by the page, she sings, she stops as we read of her waves by the edge of the sea. The road is turning plastic, pebbles it is a sunset. Moistening each page in turn with a fingertip touched to his lips, the fool of the red devisor blade. They walked then parallel and away from each other. We see them bland, sigh day. They seem to sign, their own fate in pops from vending machinery. You see they are feeling salty. They say they are foolish, wanton shell cases tossed down. Top plan of the Viet Nam Lawn. Tools in rabbit hutches. The links between cigarette lighters. Soft core yawns and ships ground down to rare earths at the bottom of the Gobi. I smiled and the mechanism was automatic. She yawned and the lots made way for schools. All men are fools, women too. Would you say so. Could you think not. The cat came out of the bar, watchers unawares. The pig escaped, but after a while. The man at the window worried in embarrassment over peeing at an angle. Red flags on blue docks in green dusk lights. Tell me about yourself in echo.

Incident of pictures shot at sharp angles. Didn't you talk with him? No. Didn't he want to talk with you? Yes, he wanted to but he didn't. Thus nothing but this now and me telling you. Twenty pounds of shrapnel flattened him. Thought to have been dotted in in pencil on the data-quarters wall. In junior highschool they had wanted their teachers caught in a crossfire in the corridor on the way to algebra or print. And drew the cartoons to prove it. Ever since the Second War a dotted line had meant death.

He smiled staring at the sun on his watch blade.
The jungle was composed of insect.
The heart a flight of jars.

XXVII

THREE MEN WERE IN THE ROOM. One took off his head, as he said, "I'm quite used to playing without my head". Another removed three eyeglass lenses from a pocket and promptly screwed them into the brass openings in a tabletop. The third man leaned a lead stick against a wall and then himself leaned back against the walls of a corner. Flakes of sunlight scattered across the room in the patterns of windblown leaves outside the french doors. A spider ran up one corner of the ruin marble fireplace, then started down again but vanished. The ceiling seemed lower than it had a few minutes earlier. A fine whitish powder evenly covered the top of one of the three tables in the room. On the wall the most in shade hung a tiny pieta, possibly of the School of Provence. Birds have an interesting history, especially previous to the 19th Century when they began to be described. Reptiles next and finally the Insecta. A large hardback novel, title illegible, with a cover depicting cumulus clouds heavily inscribed in charcoal, treats of the final destiny of the species. Faucets have the usual history. The current had been cut off and the study of fluids suffered a considerable setback. The sun was reduced to the size of a pin point, the cutglass vase inexorably moving into shadow. Music had not yet been invented. Speech was felt to be the final solution.

The hand that had trembled before the knob, the streets themselves vibrating under the military hardware, now closed the lid of the box. Wood lacks the suddenness of metal. Glass . . . No final word yet on that. Flesh being the matter in between. The cursive girl, unlocking the door of the tenement, looks up three flights to the exact window the while. She is suitably noted. A tree that bothered my mind came down under my own efforts to dismiss it. And the dinosaur dances so slowly over backwards to the floor.

What is the destiny of my intentions for these words? Yes, I do stretch in my chair to increase the field of my nerves again. I am engrossed, I think thick. The spaces being filled, no more room? The resistance of a wall of books, a well of breaths. A painter dies, I want to see all the dross that remains, the mistakes that might lead. The holes in the arrows, the bells of the corners. I want to reach out a hand in diminish of the animals that foolish me. Always the sensation that I draw my breath *in between.* Everything that could not be seen.

XXVIII

THE ONE GETS MARRIED AND GOES AWAY, the other stays in the home. I have no handwriting to speak of, I am cold. I think of things, better. The walls are partly of trees to the distance. There is no disgrace, a party to blame, there is parting. There are smokes that look like clouds. There are better ideas, and returns. There is a face that always remains, at the same distance.

I have loved those ranging messes, when the words tighten into bolts. They are my charm. My chasm is a lean lawn, or a drawn chin? Did I mean to say just that, or where did it come? I address who? Do I see my own stand in these festering rates? Am I mild, and choose action? The bed is warmer than the fingers.

The world is gradually removed in catastrophe. What was here, gone today. Tomorrow is a simple refrigerator, or stove with a screw loose. We'll have to take a look. I have constructed of course before, absolutely, my own headache. They say there are more bugs now than I remember. Just turn on the tape recorder and let in the rain. I could never have been a lawyer, I never have anything prepared to say. Sometimes I will say things that make others uncomfortable. He said to me, Don't say that. We were at night in the parking lot and the light was like a news shot after the crime. The one who was the whole point of us all being there had just left.

I suppose nothing makes any more sense (trouble) than it has to or can. I put on a tie, sometimes, but at rare intervals. Everything is alive, but some of it waits. Sometimes you get a bad smoke, it tastes of cheap perfume. I think the downhill whine of the chainsaw is now a preface. A single cello in a clear room would sound like an ancient battle.

This is a late chapter in the story of a man who has held his breath and handled doorknobs, held cold bottles of clear green liquid aloft in the sunlight, smoked away long nights over partial texts, and written in exasperation at the smallness of the attempt. Was the story of old women inserting doorknobs to keep their wombs from dropping one that Melville was not allowed to tell? Where is it written that I must await or follow anything? After all this my hand should shake, why doesn't it?

Somewhere he is enjoying his honeymoon on an island while the rest of us have all returned to our marriages in buildings. My mother had asked me my thoughts of God and all I could think of was an elegant circuitry composed of an unknown matter. In such visual times why have we lost hold of our images? The movies nothing but a progression of dates. The last stop merely the next.

XXIX

One could speak of a Cheese Auction. Under cracking beams or perhaps in the last century under parasols when no one needed much more than a fizz, in our photographs. There is cruelty. For there to be justice there must be more than one stop on a section and those two or more smacked up against eachother, an unconformity. The space between I now see is more and more active, itself the point. Down the sides of the earth it pours, a sign of time. Trujillo was not properly disposed. To tell the truth, I can see nothing but the moving sticks. It is later.There is no future.

There is fracture, or too rapid modulation, a knife between the fuckers. Over the glass an amber film gradually descends. Inside the oven a glove begins to rise. The bodies find they cannot completely separate, a tongue stuck to the frozen iron of a pump handle. Here I break out a cigarette wondering why my stomach is so sour. Brass, perhaps, or pewter. Schoenberg said a note is perceived by its color, one of whose dimensions is pitch. I imagine placing my hand inside my body cavity, assuring myself. The bodies on the bed shift and breathe, sharing the one inside.

Cold cereal but brewable morning. A tap on the shade, the skin of a violin, at rest but still under the tension. Since I cannot see it I must imagine a body of water from this window. A descending hillside, basin without the bowl. The stars are hidden by light. The troops have retreated leaving tied parcels containing their worn out shoes. The glass is as empty as a locked door.

What did we see when we emerged from the film. How did we view the lamplit street. I noticed that none of us hurried. As the children grow older the Halloween bags grow smaller. Didn't you want any more? Didn't it seem more possible all the time that the number of things you had yet to see grew greater than those you had already seen. Film as an emptying mechanism, a longer day till the end of a life? And if you decided to move faster? We bid our friends farewell under the bulbs in sequence and turn away from shock at the last report. There is a problem with the current supply, the outer regions flicker according to no particular order but do not go out.

Walking out again into daylight there is an overlapping of the false colors, a gentle wave of breathing from instrument to instrument. How does one stay alive, continue to appear in the one set of clothes? An overnight sensation, a leaving of the door on the latch. The bottle is drunk from the top down, the words in reverse as they fade from speech of memory. How long in the light of the yard at the back will the tenement poles remain. The outer regions of a chord carry the theme, holding the light a little longer. But this time we listen from the heights of the tree.

How long, O Lord, O Mind, O Thing in Motion. Sea backing 'round a point, boots leaving diamonds in the loam, volumes slicing shelves to no order. The world's types of face, stirs of plant, bolts of stone. The war was found to cease in a weak blow before the very door. No one within to see to say a thing. A novel to be written of the wendings of the jar and rejected out of hand by the printers of further time. The pages crimped and stuffed within, readied for the sea but forgotten, placed on a shelf, later to be smashed on the marble inlay floor of the Bowling Museum, Providence, 1988, no convention, no more nights of Chablis.

XXX

There's enough oil left in it to run a circus. Enough crystalline lining to air the whole outdoors. Are the animals loose? I approached the horse, startled for the rest of my life. A bomber nacelle was protruding from it in the glare of the cracked wide hill. I fastened my cap, retrieved my bike from the ivy and fled to what end of my fate. It's a meander, and leads me to a closeup of the background. The papered shelves and closet shoes and mineral packets come through with age. The stain is the life, used apparent again. Floodlit, at the angle of a building you didn't notice. It tells you nothing dangerous, an image. To be placed without force next to all the other brightening transparencies. From this will come the many relations, which do you wish?, choose. A ship on fire by a school of brick. An orchestra playing to the swamp gas. A hand that almost touches you at the swiftly closing door. The study is a retreat. With diminishing strength the story will increase its hold on the worldwide members. I didn't notice anything, I was sneezing at the word.

How can you tell. The Rate Scale has been lost. The radio is a listener, the fire rumbles higher. In a word, as in a wand, if only I could tell you. But that door is weighted, hung as if by plumber, closed as by a weld. The story held up strongly on its lone words.

He sat firmly in the chair, only one of whose legs touched the floor. Charlie and the Chair, mixed members of the same stance. As life strains by, repeated as windows. His wife had grown cross at the powder on the tabletop. She raised her hands. She raised her hands.

The ticker stopped. Breathing. Cooking. Scowls. The children were out. They had caroled down the hillside in the dark and were gone. The cat neared the door, but from the outside soon to scratch. Admit. Admit it in. What are you saving, they meant when they asked, How are you doing. And how much do you reckon now is left. How many further turnings to the story. Outside the building was a tremendous explosion, and inside a quiet of no one longer waiting. Pretend, then. Imagine and fill. You can't live further in an emptying chamber. A creak then, or a crack. But the more I arrange for a time grows sparser. Soon the lights on the hill will be farther apart.

What do I know, or equally, how do I look. Jump-cutting made of the blaming face a confession. A great deal of distance instantaneously rhymed. The slamming of the door cast broad on the hill, once shut within you can never return. She was naked, though only her vast face was visible. Don't you see how you are seeing what you are only allowed to see? Enough light but never sufficient room. The lie is what's just visible at the edge, the corner. The face in the crowd you can't stop seeing throughout the rest of the game. Those lips that will never press the opening you must gain. She will never speak again, though the film be rerun. The light has gone out in the following sentences.

Do you choose to be the one who will arrive too late for what must transpire. Will you present me with an edge on the situation. Do you know your name before you are born. Am I too old to learn clarinet. The message was neither passed beneath the door nor thrown over the transom. The car will not stop despite the level of your voice. The room will not be held at your fancy. Who is saying this? Who is reading aloud to himself? Who will turn down the radio so to inhabit the silence of the phone the better? Only the vision grows louder, as the room will cease to contain.

His mind was not on, but his hand was on the throttle. It was on the button. As the bulb hung crookeder in the aging chamber. I consider lights to be bugs and sweep them off. Why is neon a candle of ice lit always from within only in the hollows of the Nevada night? Someone there to see it, I don't think so. They only want to be in the business, devices of no need to give. Let's have a bite. Will you stand me that much. Cement to the very deal.

XXXI

THE JAR COULD BE FILLED TO THE STOPPER almost airless with fine fragments of the ancient pottery ground under the wheels of the traitors' vehicles. This is known. This is not known in the corresponding state. I lifted the hammer, I did not see it fall. I bent my brow to the Egyptian Grammar, one by Gardener, and saw the man advancing with one arm raised. Now everyone was milling in the space between the old pyramid and the one under construction, their lives in control. The task, deification of the empty space. A man raises his hand to shout, the arrangement to be completed. Their bodies the axes of a crystal sky. This is the reason for the void being blue. Among, at the last, not a single other thing.

1XII79—31X80

750 copies of this book
printed July 1982 at the
West Coast Print Center, of which
10 copies are numbered in roman
numerals i–x and signed
by the author.

THE FIGURES

Rae Armantrout *Extremities* $2.50
Paul Auster *Wall Writing* $3.00
David Benedetti *Nictitating Membrane* $3.00
Steve Benson *As Is* $5.00
Alan Bernheimer *Cafe Isotope* $3.00
John Brandi *Diary from a Journey to the Middle of the World* $4.00
Summer Brenner *From the Heart to the Center* $3.00
Summer Brenner *The Soft Room* $4.00
David Bromige *My Poetry* $6.00
Laura Chester *My Pleasure* $3.00
Laura Chester *Watermark* $4.00
Tom Clark *Baseball* $6.50
Clark Coolidge *The Crystal Text* $10.00
Clark Coolidge *Melencolia* $3.50
Clark Coolidge *Mine: The One That Enters the Stories* $7.50
Michael Davidson *The Prose of Fact* $5.00
Lydia Davis *Story and Other Stories* $5.00
Christopher Dewdney *Spring Trances in the Control Emerald Night & The Cenozoic Asylum* $5.00
Johanna Drucker *Italy* $3.50
Barbara Einzig *Disappearing Work* $4.00
Norman Fischer *On Whether or Not to Believe In Your Mind* $7.50
Kathleen Fraser *Each Next* $4.00
Gloria Frym *Back to Forth* $4.00
Merrill Gilfillan *River Through Rivertown* $4.00
Lyn Hejinian *Writing is an Aid to Memory* $4.00
Paul Hoover *Idea* $7.50
Fanny Howe *Introduction to the World* $5.00
Bob Perelman *a.k.a.* $5.00
Bob Perelman *The First World* $5.00
Bob Perelman *7 Works* $3.50
Tom Raworth *Tottering State* $11.50
Tom Raworth *Writing* $10.00
Stan Rice *Some Lamb* $4.00
Kit Robinson *Down and Back* $3.00
Stephen Rodefer *The Bell Clerk's Tears Keep Flowing* $12.00 (Cloth)
Stephen Rodefer *Four Lectures* $7.50
James Schuyler *Early in '71* $2.00
Ron Silliman *Tjanting* $10.00
Julia Vose *Moved Out on the Inside* $4.00
Guy Williams *Selected Works 1876-1982* With an Essay by Gus Blaisdell $10.00
Geoffrey Young *Subject to Fits* $5.00